The Land Between Us

The Land Between Us

Brenda O'Bannion

Tranquility Press, 2022

Tranquility Press
723 W University Ave #300-234
Georgetown TX 78626
TranquilityPress.com
TranquilityPress@gmail.com

This book is a work of fiction. Historical figures are used fictitiously, and any scenes, situations, incidents, or dialogue concerning them are not to be inferred as real. Any other similarity to real persons, living or dead, is entirely coincidental and not intended by the author.

ISBN: 978-1-950481-34-7
Library of Congress Control Number: 2021953404

Publisher's Cataloging-in-Publication data

Names: O'Bannion, Brenda, author.
Title: The land between us / by Brenda O'Bannion.
Description: Georgetown, TX: Tranquility Press, 2022.
Identifiers: LCCN 2021953404 |
ISBN (trade) 978-1-950481-34-7 | ISBN (e-Book) 978-1-950481-35-4
Subjects: West Virginia (WV). | The great depression. | Farming. | Family. |
BISAC / Historical / General. | GSAFD: Historical fiction. | LCGFT: Novel
Classification: LCC PS3620.O33665 L36 2022 | DDC 813/.6—dc23

To Mike

for the miles you drove
and the hours you listened

The Lord is near the brokenhearted
and saves the crushed in spirit. Psalm 34:8

Chapter 1

*S*hort on time, Will still felt pulled. The sun barely peeked over Bald Mountain when he stepped off the front porch, careful not to spill his morning coffee. He walked past his barn, then beyond the apple house to his favorite place—the orchard.

He lifted his eyes to gaze at the pink and white blooms that clung to the end of every branch, each with the promise of shiny, firm apples come fall. Some blooms, finished with their pollination work, now lay on the ground. Others twirled loosely before falling from their twig as he watched. "Apple snow," Grandpa Parson had called it.

Will marveled at the pure sensation of standing under one of his apple trees. His six-foot-four frame made it easy to pick the high-hanging fruit come harvest time, but more difficult to reach the apples on limbs closer to the ground. Still, he wouldn't change his job as an apple farmer. He loved the rhythm and beauty of watching seasons change as nature took its course through each year.

The drone of bees hummed in Will's ears and he glanced to the wooden hives at the edge of the orchard. *It's a wonder how those tiny creatures can cross-pollinate the whole orchard.* Without the bees, his trees would have to depend on the fickle wind to bring an apple crop each year.

He stepped between the rows of gnarly apple trees to a place he frequented when in the orchard. Standing at the fence along the edge of his farm, Will examined the bare eighteen acres on the other side. The land could expand his orchard, giving him a bigger harvest to sell. Much as he loved his orchard, it didn't produce enough apples to pay all the bills.

Applewood Orchard had been in the family for four generations. Great-grandfather Wilton Parson crossed the country in a covered wagon with a new bride, thirty seedling apple trees from his father's farm, and lots of grit. He secured the twenty acres Will now owned in 1857, when the land in West Virginia sold dirt cheap. With Will's determination, the orchard would remain in Parson hands for many generations to come. If he could only make it pay.

Standing beneath his trees, each adorned with the beauty of the blooming season, his eyes roamed the acres across the fence, planning how to plant the seedlings and where to place each variety of apple tree to get the best cross-pollination. After a few moments, he stepped back. *Best not put the cart before the horse.*

He made his way to the farthest corner of the orchard along his back boundary, where the land gave way to hills filled with large trees and a wide variety

of wildlife. Eventually this land would end at the New
River, small branches of it bringing Will's land much
coveted water.

Tucked in the corner where his land ended and
the forest began, Will stopped at three small markers.
He removed his hat and dropped his chin. The tiny
mounds of earth were no larger than a breadbox, each
marked by a small cross, each with a different a date.
As his eyes landed on the most recent, less than six
months back, he whispered a brief prayer. *Please don't
let there be any more crosses here.*

The tightness of the cap back on his head
reminded Will of his need for a haircut. He never
gave much thought to his mass of dark hair, but when
his cap grew snug over the waves and curls, he made
time to go into Sam's barbershop in Berkley. He'd once
asked Sybil to trim it for him, but her response had
been a surprised look with an emphatic, "Heavens no!
Why would I ever want to do that?"

Back at the house, Will eased open the screen
door, hoping to not wake Sybil, though little seemed
to disturb her. He wondered what his mom, who rose
before daylight her entire life, would think of a wife
who rarely appeared before noon. He took the stairs
two at a time, careful to avoid the squeak in the middle
of each step created from decades of feet traveling up
and down the staircase.

At the top, he walked past the bedroom he shared
with his wife to the second bedroom. On the bed
lay his only suit, one of his two dress shirts, and a
tie which once belonged to his father. He'd carefully
laid out his clothes the night before so he could dress
without bothering Sybil.

Will cringed at how he always had to walk on eggshells, careful not to upset his wife of four years. So different from what he imagined married life would be. Yet only a small sacrifice compared to the pain and disappointments Sybil suffered. His recent visit to the crosses flew through his mind. He pushed the thought back. Best to think only of the chore before him.

Downing a quick second cup of coffee, Will decided against breakfast, not wanting to add to his already queasy stomach. He steered his nine-year-old 1920 International Modal A truck north at the end of his driveway to make the twenty-mile trip to Berkley. On the eastern side of West Virginia, the Appalachian Mountains lay to his west and the purplish haze of the Blue Ridge Mountains rose in the east.

He glanced at the Rhode estate as he passed. They were his nearest neighbors, though not the kind you would say is neighborly in any sense of the word. Not that his mother didn't try. She'd made plenty of trips to the home of Carl and Eleanor Rhode carrying a fresh apple pie or a jar of honey.

Will's father, James Parson, chided his wife for her efforts, saying, "Leave them be. They're just uppity. One look at that big plantation home oughta tell you they ain't interested in the likes of us." More times than Will could remember, he'd heard his father's spew bitter words about Carl Rhode.

Driving past the sprawling estate, Will replayed all the things his father said so many times before his death—uppity, money-mongers, lazy, no-good rich kids, everything handed to them. He sighed as traveled the two-lane winding road through the foothills to First Security Bank, the business passed down to Carl

Rhode Jr. from his father, to ask for a loan to buy the eighteen acres next to Applewood Orchard.

Carl had a head for money and a heart for little else other than ensuring his standing in the community—a community beholden to him for loans he approved as president of the bank. Whether it was a lost job, a sick child, or a failed crop, desperate families went to Carl for help. Carl attached a large interest rate to the loans, and he never hesitated to foreclose on a farm or a small business when the debt wasn't paid back according to strict deadlines.

Fear shot through Will's body as it had so many times over the past week. *Should I risk Applewood Orchard just to have more?*

Chapter 2

*T*illy watched as the truck turned off the long driveway and dropped out of sight, then moved her gaze to the apple orchard. Her chest squeezed tight, as though someone had put it in a vise. *Be it best to not visit the past.*

She spun back to the forest and continued to forage for the plants and roots which had become her lifeline since her grandmother, Big Mama, died. The abundance of flora in the forest of the Appalachian Mountains offered a wide variety of herbal remedies for everything from the blues to hurtin' bones. Without her remedies, she'd have nothing to barter for the things she couldn't afford to buy.

Just shy of five feet two, Tilly often found valuable plants someone taller might have missed. Ebony skin and dark hair helped her blend in with the surrounding forest. Her limited wardrobe of men's dark pants and shirts served to further camouflage her existence. A pair of worn boots finished Tilly's daily clothing and added to the illusion of being male—something Big Mama said was important.

Tucked away in a chest in her cabin lay a long skirt made of blue cotton and a white, billowy blouse. Tilly heard the softness in Big Mama's voice the day she brought them to the cabin. "Someday you'll wear these, Tilly. Be patient 'til life makes its way back to you."

Hurrying to make the best of the mid-day light on the forest floor, Tilly zig-zagged through the trees searching for foxglove, witch hazel, mayapple, butterfly weed, beebalm, and peppermint.

"No cohosh in my basket this time. I sure don't need to add to the heaviness in my heart today." Tilly spoke to no one except herself.

She continued, following an invisible path to her cabin. Three and a half decades of calling it home had made the forest a second skin to Tilly. She moved among the dense lushness with the stealth of a deer.

By the time the roof of her cabin came into view, Tilly's basket all but overflowed with the fruits of her labor. Once again, she wished for a dog who would greet her back home. A thousand times she'd entertained the thought of getting one, only to dismiss it as far too dangerous.

"Don't let nobody know you live here, Tilly. Them Rhodes would never let you be. I don't reckon I could stand for you to be sent away." Three decades after Big Mama's words, Tilly's body still filled with fear at the thought of being sent away.

She paused at the edge of her clearing, letting the forest hide her for a moment, then surveyed the cabin and its surroundings for any signs of intruders. Curtained on all sides by tall pines, spruces, and red oaks, an untrained eye might miss the log structure.

Tilly knew her home so well she could maneuver inside with ease, even in the dark. The small cabin had only one door, in the middle of the south wall. The roof sloped down on the door side, resulting in the semblance of a porch. There were two windows across the front and one on each of the sides. The north wall had no windows, an effort to keep out the cold. Inside, a wood-burning stove provided both warmth and a top to cook on.

A sink with a hand pump dominated a tiny cabinet. In the middle of the room, a small table and one chair gave evidence of a single resident. The only other items were a small bed pushed against the north wall and a rocker placed by the stove in the winter and near the door in the summer.

A small shed about half the size of the cabin leaned against the back wall. From inside, Tilly could hear the rushing waters of New River. She spent much of her day here, working with her remedies.

Satisfied all was well, Tilly entered the cabin and placed the basket on the table. She waited for her eyes to adjust to the dimness, then began a methodical walk around the inside.

"Where you be, Solomon? I see you ain't bothered yourself none to fix us lunch. You 'bout the laziest ole turtle I ever knowed." Tilly continued her search, stopping in front of the stove. "There you be. What you been up to this morning? Brung you some nice stilt grass."

After a quick meal of poke salad and stale

cornbread, Tilly made her way to the shed. She worked for the rest of the afternoon to sort, bundle, and hang the abundance of plants in her basket. Next, she turned her attention to grinding the bundles she'd already dried.

She ground the dried plants in a mortar and pestle that had once belonged to her great-grandmother, Emmaline Burkes. Emmie spent her days preparing medicinal remedies and selling them to neighbors and others in the community where she lived. She passed her knowledge and tools on to her daughter, Big Mama. When Big Mama came to work for the Rhodes, years ago, she brought the mortar and pestle with her. After Tilly came, Big Mama shared the wisdom with her.

The only other thing Big Mama had brought was her Bible, now hidden away and never touched. Growing up, Big Mama read the Bible to Tilly every night and took her to church on Sunday mornings and again on Sunday nights. Tilly loved the singing and the preaching, and over time, she felt her faith grow. That changed on a single afternoon many years earlier.

Cain't say me and God get along now. Fact be, I got to wonder if he ever loved me. Seems like he oughta watched over me better.

With the grinding process complete, Tilly carefully measured the powdery substance into small medicinal bottles on which she wrote the herb's name. She would need to get more bottles soon. *How many times do I tell 'em to send back those empty bottles, but they never do.*

Tilly turned to see Solomon coming through the shed's door. "Oh, now you want to work? Well, don't be coming in here thinkin' I'm gonna give you some work. Nobody touches my plants but me." She gave her first smile of the day as she watched the turtle's slow, deliberate movements.

She'd been eternally grateful the day that turtle crawled into her clearing and walked straight to her door like he'd finally come home. She never tried to restrain him, knowing he'd need to go back to the river from time to time. Sometimes he'd leave for a day, sometimes two or three, but he always returned. When he came back, Tilly treated him to the stilt grass she kept fresh in her root cellar.

"You know, Solomon, I ain't sure if you be male or female. Just named you Solomon 'cause I 'member Big Mama telling me the story 'bout a man with that name who lived a long, long time. Hope you do the same. It'd be some lonely without you."

The late afternoon shadows stole the light from the shed, forcing Tilly to stop work. She grabbed Solomon and closed the door behind her. Before entering the cabin, she went down into the root cellar for a potato, carrot, turnip, and a few wild onions—fixings for a meatless stew. Tomorrow she would need to do some hunting for a rabbit or a squirrel.

When the kerosene lamp went out, moonlight cast shadows across Tilly's body as she sat in the rocker. Memories assaulted her, threatening to snare her in the past. She pushed them down for now, but come bedtime, she'd become their prey.

Chapter 3

*W*ill always enjoyed the drive through the Appalachian Mountains. He knew every curve and hill between Applewood Orchard and his hometown of Berkley, West Virginia. So well, in fact, he often turned his mind from driving to the beautiful fields, which gave way to the haze of mountains rising in the distance. The view usually filled his heart with gratitude for the place he called home. Today, the drive seemed long as he marked off each mile between him and the chore which lay ahead.

If only Sybil would come to appreciate our home as much as I do. He'd been so sure she'd love Applewood Orchard and Berkley as much as he did. At first, she seemed delighted with the town, the orchard, and the nineteenth-century farmhouse. Even the beekeeping fascinated her—until the first time Will took her to harvest honey. The buzz of thousands of bees sent her back to the truck in a stream of cuss words.

These days, a constant litany of whining came from Sybil. She complained about everything from the house being outdated and drafty to the twenty-mile drive to town. Will tried hard to please her, but always seemed to miss the target. The arguments were the worst. He winced, remembering their latest, brought about by Sybil's unhappiness with their lack of funds. *But maybe, just maybe, she'll be happy if I can make more profit when I enlarge the size of Applewood Orchard.*

Topping the last hill before entering Berkley, Will shook his head to clear his thoughts. He focused on the town, taking in sights he'd seen his entire life. Farthest from the square, Berkley Coal Mine rose from the side of Old Bald Mountain. Company houses, owned by the mining company and only available to those men who worked in the mine and their families, dotted the foothills just below it.

Storefronts lined the streets around a town square, a grassy place with a small gazebo and benches set under large, shady oaks. Old men arrived there each day to discuss politics, and teenagers met there at night to hold hands and sneak a kiss. Children played tag on the grass while their mothers gathered nearby to catch up with the latest town gossip.

Drivers drove around the square at a snail's pace, mindful of children at play. Most of the storefronts looked the same, with painted wood, modest single-door entries, and the shop name painted on the windows. Owners hauled a sampling of goods out to the sidewalk each day, weather permitting.

The bank emerged as the most prominent structure on the square. Built of red brick, the two-story edifice dominated everything around. It occupied the northwest corner of the square, with the name FIRST SECURITY BANK boldly displayed above the large double doors at the entry. No paint on these tall windows—instead, small half-curtains made of thick, dark green fabric could be seen from the outside.

Will fell in line with the other vehicles as they made a trip around the square like a slow-moving train. His mind rambled with the things he planned to say to Carl Rhode. Words to convey his vision for Applewood Orchard. He'd worked hard for the last eight years to bring the orchard back to a productive enterprise, something his father had shown little interest in doing.

James Parson preferred chasing rainbows over orchard keeping. He spent most of Will's childhood seeking get-rich quick schemes and drinking away his disappointment when they failed. In the end, his drinking killed him when his car hit a tree on a stormy night after a three-day binge. Will's mother had pleaded for James to stay home, saying the weather was much too dangerous for him to be driving in. But he was out of liquor and determined to have more. Five hours later, a rain-soaked chief of police knocked on their door.

After the funeral, Will's mom asked him to walk in the orchard with her. "This place is yours now to do with as you please. Sell it if you're tired of the hard work on this farm. But if you want to continue Applewood Orchard, then let's do it right. There's a horticultural school in Lynchburg. I've enough saved to pay the tuition. It's a one-year school where you'll learn about caring for land and how to make this orchard productive again."

She stopped to give Will time to absorb her words before continuing. "It's your decision, son. I'll respect whatever you want. Just give it some thought."

In the end, Will went to the school, and he never once regretted it. He learned ways to make the apple orchard come to life again. And before the year ended, he'd fallen head over heels in love with Sybil.

A horn startled Will out of his thoughts. He'd made his way around the square and arrived at the front of the bank. He eased his truck into a parking spot near the front door, straightened his tie, and got out.

Inside, he let his eyes adjust to the dim yellow globe lights hanging from the tall ceiling of the large lobby. To his right, customers stood in a quiet line before the cashier's window, waiting to make a transaction.

Random thoughts flew around Will's head as he reflected on the bursting economy. Prosperity abounded around the country since the end of the Great War. *They're probably making a deposit.* Encouraged that today's visit might be fruitful, he turned to the desk on his left.

"I...ahem." It embarrassed him when his voice squeaked like a thirteen-year-old boy. He cleared his throat and tried again. "I'm here to see Mr. Rhode."

"Name?" The young lady kept her eyes on the typewriter, her lacquered red nails clicking out words with amazing speed.

"Will Parson."

When she finally looked up at Will, the clacking stopped as her hands froze over the typewriter. She stared at his face, moved her sight down to his feet, then leveled her gaze on his eyes. Her bright red lips parted into a seductive smile.

"Well, hi there, Will Parson. Let's see if we can find you in his calendar."

Will's hands curled tight around the edge of his hat. *I should have known to make an appointment.* He opened his mouth to tell her to not bother to look at the appointments when she spoke again.

"Well, sugar, I don't see your name here, but I'll bet I can work you into his morning. I'll just pop into Carl's, uh, Mr. Rhode's, office and see what I can do to get him to see you. By the way, my name's Molly—Miss Molly Wagner."

Will mumbled his thanks as she entered a large door behind her desk. After a moment, he realized he stood in front of an empty desk. Glancing around, he retreated to a chair against the wall.

Molly returned several minutes later, tucking a few strands of hair into the pinned coif at the nape of her neck.

"Good news, Will. He'll see you, but you may have a bit of a wait. He's very busy right now."

"Thank you, Miss Wagner. I appreciate it."

"Call me Molly. Most men do."

For the next hour, Will sat in the chair, trying not to notice the many trips Molly made to her file cabinet to bend over to the bottom drawer, her tight skirt all but exploding. Or her frequent trips to water plants around the lobby, her heels clacking like her typewriter. All his instincts told him to stay far away from this woman named Molly.

Seventy-five slow, agonizing minutes passed. Will returned his hat to his head and stood to leave when the intercom on Molly's desk buzzed.

"He'll see you now, Will. It's been nice to have a little company this morning." Her deep red lips parted into a huge smile as if Will was a lost friend just returned.

Will rounded her desk and entered through the door to find himself in a large, ornately decorated office with tall windows facing the town square.

"Come in, Will." Carl pointed to a chair directly in front of his voluminous oak desk. "Sorry to keep you waiting, but I've been on the phone with the mayor. I swear, he never seems to make a move without first calling me. I've got a little time now. What brings you to town?"

Every word Will had so carefully rehearsed for the past few days flew out of his head. He stammered something about the farm and his desire to grow more apple trees. He rattled on, barely making a coherent sentence, when Carl interrupted him.

"Well, if I'm following your thoughts, you're looking to buy more land. And I suspect you're here to ask for a loan. Let me make this short, for both our sakes. There is no land around your place that's for sale, and even if there were, this bank would never make a loan against Applewood Orchard. Just not good collateral." He paused as he replaced the cap on the end of his pen and placed papers in his desk drawer. "Now, if you'll excuse me, I've got a businessman's meeting to attend. Hell, not attend. Run. I've been the president of the club for the past three years." Carl grinned as if he'd said something impressive.

Will stood, amazed at how quickly he'd been brushed off. "But what about the land between us? I assume it's a foreclosure since the Trevors left so quickly. I thought your bank held their note."

The smile plastered on Carl's round, puffy face disappeared. He rose from his chair to grab his suit jacket off a coatrack. "I don't make it a habit to discuss bank business with someone who isn't a holder in this bank. The answer is no, Mr. Parson. No loan. Now, I must leave. I can't be late for my meeting."

Stunned by the banker's rudeness, Will watched as Carl Rhode rushed from his office. Confusion and defeat battled in his chest as he exited the office and walked past the secretary without a word.

Chapter 4

Eleanor lifted the lid from a simmering pot and a cloud of steam engulfed her face. She stirred the ingredients, taking in the comforting aroma of chicken noodle soup. Her lips curved into a bitter-sweet smile. Danny's favorite soup, made today because of the scene the night before. The smile melted as she remembered the hateful words from Carl and the hurt look on Danny's face when rebuked by his father.

Wiping the moisture off her face with her apron, she made her way through the ornate dining room to a foyer as large as her parent's home back in Pineville. She never moved through the large entryway of their home without thinking of her parents. More love lived in their small home than in all the planks combined of the eighteenth-century plantation home Carl had brought her to as a bride almost twenty-four years ago. She shook her head, reminding herself that love lived in this home—the love of a mother and a son. She never quit praying that the same love would somehow make its way into the hearts of her husband and her oldest son, Johnny.

Eleanor stepped out on the long porch and lifted her hand to shield her eyes from the sun as she searched the riding pasture next to the house. She saw Danny on his favorite mare, Sunshine, with their horse trainer leading the reins around the track. Every day the weather permitted, Sam helped Danny onto the saddle, then walked him around the track as many times as the young man wanted, giving no care for all the work he had waiting in the stables. She often saw a light in the stables late at night as Sam labored to finish the work he'd set aside for Danny.

How many times had Eleanor thanked God for this kind, generous man—the only man Eleanor had ever seen go against Carl. When Carl forbade Sam to help Danny ride, the trainer told him flat-out he intended to give this time to Danny. Carl would have fired him on the spot, but Sam was the best trainer in West Virginia. Without him, Carl's reputation as a horseman would not be as strong. And in her husband's mind, this meant money. Enough money to overlook an employee who might dare go against him.

Eleanor waved from the porch. "Hello, Sam. Time for Danny's lunch. I imagine you're ready for some yourself."

"I am at that, Miz Rhode. Only thing that's been louder than my stomach this past hour is Danny's constant talking!" Sam slowed the mare to a stop and pulled a bandanna from his back pocket to wipe his brow.

"Hi, Mama. Me and Sam been talking and riding!" Danny grinned as he slid down off Sunshine's back.

"Hey," Sam protested, "you're the only one who's been chattering like a magpie. I just been walking and listening."

Danny pulled his head back and guffawed. "You funny, Sam."

Eleanor watched her grown son as he bantered with Sam, thankful once again for the man who had befriended her disabled boy. Her mind shot back to that fateful evening twenty years ago, the day of Danny's accident.

The annual Rhode Christmas party moved in full swing when Sheriff Eakin arrived. Eleanor greeted him at the door but didn't dare linger in conversation, seeing Carl nearby and watching. "Good evening, Benson. I'm so glad you came," was all she said, though she wanted to say more when she saw the tiredness in his eyes and in the slope of his shoulders.

"I'm sorry to arrive so late, Eleanor. Problems over in the flats tonight."

Eleanor nodded but didn't ask more. She knew how closed-lipped Benson could be about his job as Briar County Sheriff.

Her husband suddenly appeared at their side. "No problem what time you get here, Sheriff, just glad you came. Although I admit, we're two or three drinks ahead of you. Let's go see if we can remedy the problem." Carl turned Benson away from Eleanor and in the bar's direction, trying without success to not limp on the leg that suffered from an old football injury.

Benson watched Carl's labored walk to join the mayor and his wife, then threw a quick glance at Eleanor. "Excuse me, please, Eleanor. Best follow the advice of my host."

Eleanor nodded, though she knew Benson wouldn't catch up with Carl's drinking. Her husband was well on his way to being drunk, something that could cause a problem if she weren't careful as the night grew old.

She left the foyer and made her way to the kitchen to check on the food. Ola Mae bustled around filling trays of delectable finger foods, then rushing her nephew out the door to serve the guests.

"Now get on out there, Otis. Them partygoers be needing some food in their stomachs or we gonna see a drunken mess for sure! And don't be spilling nothing on that white jacket."

Ola Mae watched her nephew as he entered the dining room, offering food to those standing in groups of three and four before moving on to the formal living room. She turned to Eleanor. "I proud o' that boy. He gonna grow up to a just fine man. And he smart, too. Highest math scores in the entire school. He smart, like my Desmond."

Nodding, Eleanor's heart warmed for Ola Mae's enjoyment of her nephew. Since her son died last year in an accident at Berkley Mine, Ola Mae spent much of her time grieving. The conditions in the mine were deplorable, resulting in injuries and even deaths every year. Eleanor once tried to talk to Carl about it, hoping he might bring the situation to the city council.

Instead, he berated her for talking with the help. "They should be happy to get the work."

With a sigh, Eleanor closed the heavy door behind the last guest, relieved the party had ended. She glanced into the study, where Carl slumped in his office chair in a drunken stupor, then made her way toward the stairs, walking on her tiptoes so as not to wake her husband. She rounded the corner in the foyer to start up the stairs when she felt Carl grab her hair from behind.

"I saw all those looks you and the sheriff were passing back and forth all evening. Think I'd miss that? Well, you think wrong. Should've known, can't take trash out of a trash bin and expect it to behave like us civilized folk."

He pulled tighter on her hair, drawing her closer, his breath reeking of gin and tobacco. She held still as possible, trying not to groan, which always seemed to fuel his anger. When his drunkenness caused him to stumble back a step, she seized the opportunity and raced up the stairs, hoping to get to the bedroom where she could lock the door. But Carl proved to be quicker than she expected. Eleanor screamed when he grabbed her right arm and twisted it with such force she feared it would break.

"Please, Carl, don't do this again. I've told you over and over, there's nothing between Benson and me. I knew him before we married. He once took me home from work when a storm rolled in. It meant nothing."

"Now you and I both know that's not the truth. What about when you and he were in your car? It was the time you said the vehicle stalled, and he helped you get it started. What else did he start, Eleanor? And what about the baby that came nine months later? What about that, Eleanor?" He pulled her around to face him, his face contorted with anger and disgust.

She winced at the pain shooting down her arm as she tried to calm her husband. "I've told you so many times, nothing happened. He just waited with me until the tow truck got there. And Danny was born early. We all know that by his low birth weight. Danny's yours, Carl. Please, believe me."

"If he's mine, why's his hair black? Yours ain't; neither is mine. Even Johnny has brown hair like the both of us. Explain that, Ellie from Pineville!"

Fear rose from Eleanor's gut, hurting more than the pain in her arm. He only used her actual name when he wanted to belittle her. He'd insisted she use Eleanor when he brought her to his home, saying it was more dignified for the wife of a man of his standing. She knew from past experience, when the belittling started, the abuse grew worse.

"You know your dad had black hair. Danny looks like him."

Carl responded by twisting her arm tighter and stepped on her foot with his brand-new cowboy boot. When she cried out in pain, a bedroom door opened, and the little eight-year-old walked into the hallway.

"Mama?"

Eleanor's heart sunk. "Danny, honey, go back to sleep. Daddy and I are just going to bed."

But it was too late. Danny saw his mother's tear-stained face and Carl's grip on Eleanor's arm. Without warning, he charged straight to Carl with all the strength an eight-year-old could muster. "Stop it, Daddy. Don't hurt her."

Carl kept his grip on Eleanor as he thrust out his other arm, slamming it into the charging child with such a force Danny's feet flew out from under him and he pummeled down the staircase. He landed on his head, collapsed into unconsciousness.

The familiar sound of a Model A truck pulled Eleanor out of her thoughts. She watched Will Parson roll by, headed to Applewood Orchard.

At the far end of the eighteen acres between her land and Will's, a shadow moved among the century-old oak and spruce trees.

Chapter 5

"*H*ello, girl. Did you miss me?" Will stepped from his truck after parking it in the shed and leaned over to rub the neck of his dog, Daisy.

Turning his head, he looked at the house, reluctant to go inside. How often had he come home to the intoxicating aromas of his mother's pork roast or the yeasty smell of homemade rolls just removed from the oven? His favorite scent had to be apples cooking in cinnamon and other spices—his apples.

These days, White King granulated soap flakes and strong, flowery perfume assaulted his nose every time he entered his home. Unable to muster the courage to go in the house just yet, he made his way to the apple barn, a place where he could put in the heavy labor his tight muscles were screaming for after the events of the morning.

"Come on, girl, let's see what we can work on."

Happy to be at her master's side, the yellow and white border collie matched her stride to his.

Will pushed the wide double doors open to let in natural light and breathed deeply of the sweet apple smell that never left the sixty by ninety foot tin building. Five years ago, he tried to dissuade his father from replacing the old apple barn with funds they didn't have. But James Parson charged full speed ahead, building a top-of-the-line structure. He'd used all their small savings and financed the rest at a high interest rate.

One side wall held shelves full of picking baskets. A collection of ladders leaned against the opposite wall. In the middle, a long table with a three-inch ledge on all four sides served to sort the apples before packing them. A long worktable stood along the back wall—a place to build the crates used for shipping.

This building would be the perfect size to handle both apple crops, once he acquired the orchard next to his. With apple prices down, he needed more trees to provide a harvest that would cover the farm's expenses. As things were now, even a bumper crop wouldn't carry him through the year.

A phrase played over and over in his mind, one used often by his mom. It grated on his nerves like a fingernail across a chalkboard. The day his father signed the papers for the new structure, his mom had stood in the kitchen drying her hands on her apron. While Will chided his father about the foolishness of spending money they didn't have, his mother simply stated, "The Lord will provide."

Will's frustration grew each time his father acted recklessly with the farm's management. He struggled even more when his mom seemed to think her faith could provide the answer to everything. He'd stormed out that day, driving through the back roads, burning gasoline he should have saved. He ended up near the crest of Bald Mountain, where he'd sat in his car watching shooting stars in the freezing November night. Gradually, his jaw relaxed and the strain in his neck loosened.

When he returned home, his supper sat on the stove, covered with a clean dishtowel. He ate the cold meal, then rinsed the plate and utensils, not wanting his mom to face his dirty dishes in the morning. Five years later, embarrassment of his behavior that night still caused a hard rock in his stomach.

"Daisy, apple prices had better go up before the harvest or Culvert Construction Company will show up to take this barn apart piece by piece and haul it off."

Daisy wagged her tail and looked up at him. "Woof."

Moving to the long wall where the baskets sat in stacks on shelves, Will began a careful inspection, searching for rips in the thin sweet-gum slats and tears in the webbing that held the basket in shape. Some he would mend; others he'd throw out, too damaged from last season. A quick survey informed him he would likely need to buy more baskets for the fall harvest.

After discarding the worthless baskets, Will stacked the good ones back on the shelf. He took the remaining baskets to a worktable near the barn opening. *I need to save as many baskets as possible.*

Again, he heard his mother's voice. "The Lord will provide."

He didn't provide the extra land I need, Mom. I'm hanging on by a thread here.

His stomach knotted into a tight ball as grief made an unwelcome appearance. A blizzard roared outside in the December night when his mother told him she had liver cancer. Stunned, his mind brought up the picture of the plot next to where they'd buried his father two years before. A place designated for his mother—but not for years to come, he thought. With urgency, he'd told his mom, "We'll fight this. Maybe go to Charleston. Surely there's something they can do there. We have to try, Mom."

With a quiet peacefulness, she responded, "No, son. It's in the Lord's hands now." Long into the stormy night, Will tried to reason with his mother, hearing the same response over and over. A storm as fierce as the one raging outside grew inside him.

Over the next months, Will watched the cancer rob the life from his mother. Eleven months later, she lay in the plot next to his father. Even now, three years after her death, Will's grief often took his sleep. Something else was robbed from Will as he watched the disease suck the life from his mom. He lost his faith, no longer willing to let God reign in his life as he'd been taught.

A sudden, piercing car horn near the house drew Will's attention to the yard. He started out of the barn, ready to greet the visitor, but hung back when he saw Sybil come out the door. She wore a red dress with white polka dots, which fit her like a glove. Red heels with straps around her ankles elevated her slight height.

"Hello, sugar. I'm glad to see you." Sybil's voice

purred as she leaned on the post at the top of the steps, one shoe bottom propped up the post's side.

"Hello, Mrs. Parson. You're looking mighty fine today, as always. Even extra fine in that red dress. I always love me a woman in a red dress." The man made his way to the steps carrying a large case.

Will took a step forward, riled by what this man said to his wife. But the next words stopped him in his tracks.

Sybil moved closer to the man when he got to the top step. Her red heels clacked on the wooden boards as she closed the space between them. "Oh, Everett. You make me feel so womanly. Will never notices what I have on." She laid one hand on the man's chest.

"Well, he must be blind because you're always a sight to behold."

"Oh, stop that talk and come on in. I'm dying to see what new products you brought today."

"My pleasure, Mrs. Parson."

The two disappeared into the house and soon the muffled words of the salesman and Sybil's high-pitched laugh wafted through the screen door. The surrounding air seemed to dissipate. Will walked over to a chair at the end of the sorting table and lowered himself into it, then hung his head and held it in his two hands.

Disgust filled him as he considered why he didn't approach the house and put the salesman back on the road. Maybe he'd been expecting the inevitable for a long while. He'd seen the look in the eyes of others—a look that said she'd never stay. Even his mother's body language screamed out to him, conveying the same thought. But he loved Sybil and kept the hope that she would eventually love him and Applewood Orchard enough to make their marriage work.

Memories flooded his mind. The first time he saw her, he'd left Ag Mechanics class and stopped by the college diner for a soda. There she was, sitting on a stool where the bar curved to face the front door, sipping on a strawberry shake. Her blond hair hung in long curls down her back, smaller tendrils framing her face. The blue dress, fitted to show off a near-perfect figure, made her eyes a piercing azure. The reaction he had just looking at her was unlike anything he'd ever experienced. It was like time stopped and would never reset itself in the same way again. He loved her since that moment; but was his love enough to sustain this kind of behavior?

An hour had passed and the salesman had long since left when Will stomped the dirt off his boots before stepping onto the porch. With determination, he put a smile on his face and entered his home.

"Sybil, where are you? I've been mending baskets in the apple house and..."

"Will, please don't go on and on about your apples. I have a headache. I've been here on the couch all day."

Will swung into the parlor where Sybil lay on the sofa, wearing a soft blue house dress and black open-toed shoes. "You've been on the couch all day, Sybil?"

"That's what I just said. Please don't make me repeat myself. It makes my head hurt worse."

Anger coursed through Will's body like a bullet through a rifle. Sybil's most recent lie, heightened by his cowardly response to the scene on the porch, left him with no restraint. He had a sudden desire to lash out, to make her feel as badly as he did.

"Sybil, I went to the bank in Berkley today to see about a loan to buy the orchard next to ours." Will waited to see her reaction. "They said no. We won't be able to enlarge our apple crop. Chances are, next year will be as lean as this one has been."

Sybil jerked the cloth from her eyes and sat up so fast it made Will blink. "How can they do that? Your family has been a part of Berkley for generations. Why, your grandfather was best friends with Samuel Rhode. How dare they say no! You need to get yourself back there in the morning and make them understand. I can't live another year like this one, Will. I really can't." Her large blue eyes filled with tears as she looked at Will.

Will instantly regretted his ill-feelings. His heart squeezed when he saw her distraught face. "I'm sorry, sweetheart, but there's nothing else I can do. Not only won't they give me a loan, but the land isn't for sale."

Getting to her feet, Sybil paced from the sofa to the fireplace and back. "Of course it's for sale. Everything is for sale if the price is right. My daddy always says..." She spun around to face Will. "That's it. We'll get Daddy to loan you the money to buy the land! Why didn't I think of that before? If you walk into First Security Bank with cash, they'll sing another tune about selling. I'll write to him tomorrow."

"Sybil Parson, I'll not borrow from my father-in-law. I can take care of my wife without having to ask her father for money. No more talk about it."

"Oh, you're the most pig-headed man I've ever known. Why did I let you bring me to this backwoods farm in a one-horse town? I'm miserable, and I don't intend to spend another..." She grabbed her stomach with one hand and covered her mouth with the other. She pushed past Will and rushed down the hall to the restroom.

Will stood in the middle of the living room and listened to the telltale sounds of heaving.

Chapter 6

A loud crash sent Will rushing from the kitchen, his first cup of coffee still in his hand. "Sybil, are you okay?" Silence followed. He took the stairs two at a time, sloshing coffee with each lunge.

He turned the doorknob of the bathroom, but it wouldn't budge. "What's wrong? Why is the door locked?" He jiggled the knob while pressing his shoulder into the door. "Let me in so I can help you."

More silence. Then he heard Sybil's voice just on the other side of the door. "It's okay, Will. I'm fine, just dropped my bottle of Chanel. It's my last and who knows when I can get another in this god-forsaken place. Go on, now, and get your work done."

Her voice did little to assure him she was fine. It sounded flat and forced, like she was reading a script. He stood another moment. "All right. I'm going to the beehives. I'll check in on you before I go to the honey shed."

Sounding more like herself, Sybil replied, "No. If you're not using the truck, I think I'll go into town. Though heaven knows if I can find any decent perfume in Berkley, much less my favorite."

Will paused as he considered offering to drive her to town. Not knowing how she might react, he said, "There's a few dollars in the money can on the kitchen shelf. Drive safe, Sybil."

He glanced at the coffee stains spread across the front of his shirt as he walked into the bedroom to change. He'd learned long ago to not carry a foreign scent near his hives. Bees become aggressive over two things, odors and foul weather.

It didn't take long to grab another shirt from his closet, and he was soon downstairs making a second cup of coffee and some toast for a quick breakfast. "I'm leaving now, Sybil. Enjoy your trip to town." He waited for a response, which came as an unintelligible mumble.

Breathing deeply, Will tried to settle his frazzled nerves. Why did so many days begin like this—Sybil in a tizzy and him at a loss for how to help? It had been three weeks since Sybil threw up, three weeks waiting anxiously for his wife to announce the pregnancy. But the news never came, and Sybil was more disagreeable than ever.

In the honey shed, Will put on his one-piece beekeeper suit, designed to protect him from stings. He filled the small hand-pulled wagon with his smoker, some paper, a few matches, and his beekeeper's hood and gloves.

He took the shortest way to the hives, though he would have liked to go through the orchard. Most of the blooms were gone by now, but he loved to study the small knobs that would slowly grow into beautiful apples. The wagon was too clunky to go through the orchard, so he followed a small path from below the house to the back of the orchard.

Today Will planned to harvest the spring honey—a special variety of pale gold with a subtle apple taste. Customers requested more of the golden honey than he could provide. He'd harvest two more times this year, once in late summer and again in the fall, but those flows would have the color of tree bark with the flavor of summer wildflowers. At the final harvest he would leave some of the sweet, thick liquid for the bees to feed on over the winter.

Will left the creaky wagon several yards away from the hives so as not to disturb the bees, then tightened the cuffs of his suit at the ankles and wrists. He'd been stung enough in the past to build an immunity, but he still reacted to the sudden sharp prick, which made the bees more aggressive. After starting a fire with the paper in the smoker's belly, he pulled on his gloves and put his hat and face net into place. Ready to work, he began a slow walk to the hives, pushing the bellow of the smoker to release smoke ahead of him.

Over the years, he'd grown from one hive to five, learning how to re-queen each new hive to ensure it would fill with hundreds of bees to pollinate his apple trees and provide honey to sell. He was especially thankful for his beekeeping skills today. It required calculated, focused movements, keeping his mind away from the farm's problems and Sybil's moods.

"Okay, bees, let's play nice today." He lifted the corner of the lid on the first hive and pressed the bellow, which pushed most of the bees deeper into the hive. A few moments later, Will pulled the first flat from the hive and checked for the wax plugs that held honey in the combs. Satisfied the flat had an abundance of honey, he took it to the wagon, then came back to get more. The next two frames didn't have enough plugs to harvest. He returned them to the box and continued on to the rest of the frames.

"Ouch!" Will felt the sting on the top of his wrist when he pulled out the eighth and final frame from the top box. The clamp on this left wrist had become undone. Cursing himself for not checking his suit each time he took a frame to the wagon, he rubbed the sting, then jerked when he heard what sounded like a giggle from the woods.

"Who's there?" He scanned the wall of trees behind the hives, then took a few steps closer to the trees. There he stopped, watching and listening. He saw no one, but had the strong impression of being watched. It wasn't the first time he'd felt he wasn't alone while at the beehives. He always shrugged it off, sure it resulted from how much time he spent working alone on the farm. But this time, he knew he'd heard something.

He returned to his hives and pulled frames from the remaining hives, checking each carefully and leaving any frame not at least 80 percent covered in wax. Experience had taught him to harvest only the full ones, leaving the others for later, after the bees had completed their work.

Back in the honey shed, Will removed his suit and began cutting away the wax plugs from each frame. It was a tedious job but important, as it prevented any wax bits from getting into the honey. Next, he put each frame into the spinner and cranked the handle in a swift, round movement. He smiled as he watched the centrifugal force cause the honey to collect at the bottom of the device. After draining the last drop of honey through a spout under the extractor into a clean bucket, Will began the process of bottling the thick, golden liquid.

He smiled again when he opened the small box of handmade labels. He and Sybil made them during the long winter evenings—the one thing he and his wife did together. Will cut the labels from freezer paper, and Sybil printed "Applewood Orchard Honey" and drew a small apple tree in blossom. Now, he carefully spread glue on the back of the labels and attached one to each full jar. Soon, two dozen jars of honey were ready for sale.

Will stepped back and surveyed his labor. Then he remembered the sound from the woods. On impulse, he grabbed a jar of the honey.

Outside the shed, he walked swiftly to the back of the orchard. Once there, he placed the honey on a fallen log just inside the trees.

"If that jar is still there tomorrow, I'll know it's all in my imagination."

Chapter 7

Sybil watched Will from her bedroom window. "Look at him, going to work with those silly bees. What he should do is talk to my father about a loan." She turned from the window to grab her purse. Downstairs, she emptied the money can and crammed five ones into her purse. "This had better be enough!" She went out the back door, letting the screen door slam, and rushed to the truck.

After a few loud grinds, the engine turned over and settled into a low hum. At the end of the drive, she turned the opposite direction from Berkley. Once on the road, her speed matched her mood—urgent, determined. Ten minutes later, she turned left onto a small dirt road. After winding down the narrow lane, she arrived at River Town, a small community of poor folks who made their living fishing in the river. She drove to Josiah Smith's place, the last in a row of similar river shacks.

Barely allowing the truck to come to a stop, she jerked the keys from the ignition and scrambled from the driver's seat to stand beside the truck. "Josiah! I need to talk to you. Come here this instant!" she yelled, waiting only a second before she reached in and pounded the truck horn.

Sadie Mae stepped out the front door, wiping her doughy hands on her apron. "Child, you ain't gonna get that husband o' mine here any quicker blowin' a horn. Josiah Smith never hurried a day in his life. He down to the river, casting for bait. Reckon he be here directly," she said, then quietly disappeared into the house.

Sybil placed her hands on her hips and pressed her lips together. Desperation grew with each moment she waited. Soon, she started pacing the length of her vehicle. Ten agonizing minutes later, Josiah ambled around the side of his house carrying a bait bucket.

"Mornin', Miz Parson. You got business with me today?"

"I do, and it's urgent. I need you to go to the plant lady for some cohosh. Tell her the first didn't work. She has to give me more of it this time."

"Now, Miz Parson, I ain't s'pose to meet her again 'til next Tuesday. I go today, she ain't gonna know to meet me on the river."

"Well, you'll just have to figure it out when you get there," Sybil said as she reached inside the truck window and pulled the money from her purse. "Three dollars are for the plant lady. The other two are for you when you come back. Now, get going and don't come back without what I need." She grabbed Josiah's hand and shoved three crinkled bills into it.

Josiah shook his head and looked at the wadded dollar bills. "I try, but I ain't guaranteein' I can get her to the river."

"You better think of a way on your trip down, because I'll be right here waiting when you come back," Sybil hissed as she got into the truck.

Josiah left the bait bucket on the porch and hollered to his wife. "Sadie Mae, reckon I be makin' a trip downriver."

Sadie Mae stepped out the front door with hot biscuits wrapped in newspaper. "Give these to Tilly, and you be careful. River's high and fast with the spring melt."

Josiah smiled at his wife, grateful she never asked many questions about the plant lady. If she had, he likely wouldn't be making this trip today. "Thankee, wife. I be back soon for the rest o' this batch of good-smellin' biscuits."

The trip took only fifteen minutes in the swift current of the swollen river. When he reached the meeting place, he tied his boat to a low tree limb then stepped onto the bank. Using the signal he and Tilly had worked out years ago, he put his fingers to his lips and gave three short, high-pitched whistles, waited to the count of ten, then repeated the same. If Tilly was close by, she'd come to see him.

A few minutes later, she appeared through a grove of cottonwood trees that lined the river. "Josiah, somethin' wrong? What you doin' here today?"

"That Parson woman showed up to my house in a big tizzy. She's wantin' more cohosh. Sent ya three dollars. Says you got to give her more'n last time. Gonna give me two dollars for makin' the trip."

"You tell her she cain't have no more. If it ain't worked by now, means that little baby done took holt. More cohosh won't change it now."

"She gonna throw a hissy fit. Gots a real mean look in 'er eyes." Josiah shook his head as he prepared to leave. "Reckon I see ya next week, Miz Tilly?"

"Yes, I'll have you some joint medicine ready by then, and more tea for the woman with that stomach ailment."

"Okay. Reckon I'll go on back now and deliver the news to Miz Parson. She gonna be plenty mad." He climbed back into his boat, mumbling about the two dollars that wouldn't be in his pocket.

When he rounded the last bend before reaching his house, he saw Sybil standing on the small, rickety dock behind his house. He laid his oars across his boat, drifting to give himself time to think. "Reckon she thought she'd get me back quicker if'n she stood lookin' down river. Law, what a crazy fool," he mumbled. Sighing, he lifted his oars once more, easing his boat toward the river's edge.

"Now, Miz Parson, I knowed you ain't gonna like this, but I ain't got what you wantin'. She done say no, and they ain't nothin' I can do 'bout it," he said as he busied himself tying off his boat, unwilling to look into the woman's hard, cold eyes. "She say it be too late to work, so that's an end on it." He stepped onto the dock, fished the money out of his pocket, and laid it on an upturned bait bucket.

"What do you mean, the end of it? It's not the end

until I say so! You can just get right back in that boat and—"

"No'm, don't reckon so. I done made one trip for nothin'. Don't plan on makin' another." He turned and strolled into the back door of his house without another word.

The words from her mouth, spewed out at his back when he left her on the dock, shocked even him. Worse than he'd ever heard in a juke joint.

Josiah and Sadie Mae watched from their front window as Sybil put the truck into reverse and spun dirt and pebbles as she peeled from the driveway.

"I never heard them kind o' words comin' from the mouth o' no woman," Sadie Mae said. "She needs a mess o' Jesus. Never seen somebody so unhappy and angry. Must be a hard way to live life."

"'Spect so, Sadie," Josiah replied as he removed his fishing cap and rubbed his head with a wrinkled blue handkerchief. "Some peoples sho' can get they lives into a heap o' trouble. You gots any more them biscuits left, or did those youngins eat 'em all up?"

"Josiah Mason Smith, when did I ever not keep a biscuit for you?"

Chapter 8

*A*ngry tears made it difficult for Sybil to see the road. She banged on the steering wheel hard enough to cause red marks on her palms. *How dare that woman refuse to give me what I need! It worked the other times. Why not now?*

A sudden sharp curve and skidding tires brought Sybil's attention back to the road. She hit the brakes and held a steady grip on the wheel. The truck came to a bumpy stop, perilously close to a row of large pine trees that lined the road.

"That crazy old woman! Now she almost killed me!" More sobs rose from her chest. "Well, I won't give up. There are other ways to take care of this. I won't stop until I find a way." There on the side of the road, with no one to hear except herself, she felt the full impact of her declaration. Exhausted by the emotions of the day, she sat as still as a mouse. "I will, I will," she whispered. Spent, she finally ran out of words.

A sudden soft breeze filtered through the open car window, causing a curl of hair to come undone. It occurred to her to straighten it, but she never raised a hand. *Why bother? My face must look awful. And if I don't act soon, my figure will be a mess, too.*

Another breeze came—more like a flutter. Sybil looked around, wondering if a butterfly had flown through the window. Then she felt it again and realized it came from within her. In another moment, she knew the child had moved. Her anger melted away in the pure awe of the moment.

So different from the past times when there was only the sharp pain of cramping and a heavy flow. She never once thought of the others as being alive. And Will making those silly crosses. Not even a body to lie beneath them. She told him not to, but each time he'd insisted. "Those babies were alive and now they're not. This is a way to remember them."

In this moment, she had evidence of that very thing. A nurturing and longing like nothing she had ever felt before filled her being.

Sybil sat with her hand on her tummy and savored the moment belonging only to her and her child. Another flutter and both hands flattened across her stomach. Then two more, so subtle she'd have missed them completely had she not been sitting so still on the quiet roadside.

Slowly, like a snail creeping along a garden path, a thought came. "Maybe I can do this. Having a child might be nice. At least I'd have someone to talk to besides Will. If it's a girl, I can dress her pretty and teach her to dance." Her voice strengthened as she rubbed small circles on her abdomen. "You will be a girl—I insist."

Will stepped onto the back porch, then stopped, surprised not to hear the music of Louie Armstrong, Benny Goodman, and other jazz musicians which usually filled the house. Entering the kitchen, he glanced at the kitchen clock on the shelf above the cookstove. Four o'clock.

Is Sybil still in Berkley? There aren't enough shops to keep her there this long. He walked to the living room, expecting to see her on the couch. Not finding her, he moved up the stairs, careful to avoid the creaks in case she was asleep.

The bedroom held clothes and shoes thrown haphazardly on the bed, floor, and chest, but no Sybil. He returned to the hall and made his way to the bathroom. "Sybil, you in there? I'm finished with the honey harvest. Why aren't you playing your music?"

Silence.

When no response came, Will pushed through the door, wincing when the smell of spilled perfume hit his nose. He stepped inside and heard the crunch of glass under his boot. "Why is there glass all the way over to the door?"

His answer came when he turned around and saw a sizable chunk of missing wood high on the door with streams of dried perfume coursing down to the floor. His gut tightened at the realization of the scene before him. "Enough, Sybil. I've had enough! No more lies and no more temper fits."

Gagging from the strong perfume smell, Will picked up the glass shards and cleaned the perfume from the door and floor. He worked in small jerks, scrubbing harder than necessary.

Exhausted more from his anger than the labor, Will gathered the cleaning supplies to return to the kitchen. Halfway down the stairs, he heard the grinding sound of the truck's brakes coming to a hard stop. He sat the supplies on the kitchen table before moving to the couch in the living room. The same couch his wife had been on the last time she lied. No, not the last time. The last was today. *No more lies, Sybil. It stops now!*

Fists balled and mouth set in a hard line, Will listened for the creak of the screen door. It seemed an eternity before he heard it.

"Sybil, come in here. We need to talk," said Will, knowing full well she would bark back an excuse not to come. He raised his voice a decimal. "Come in here now. I mean to talk with you."

Sybil walked slowly into the room, eyes downcast. Will shot to his feet, surprised and concerned by her appearance. Red puffy eyes, smeared makeup, and tangled, wind-blown hair. His wife, always immaculately dressed, would have never gone to town looking like this.

He rushed toward her but she lifted her hand to stop him and said in a broken whisper, "Will, I need to tell you something."

The anger building since he entered the house dissipated like smoke rising from a fire. In its place, a fear grew in the innermost part of his being. Someone or something had hurt her. Instinct told him to use gentleness.

"Come to the couch, Sybil. Tell me what happened," he said, fighting to keep the rawness of his feelings at bay.

"You know the sharp curve, the one just past the river?" Sybil began in a tear-filled voice.

He nodded in agreement, not trusting himself to speak without screaming for her to get it out.

"I was coming back from buying my perfume in town. I must have drove too fast. The truck slid and... Oh, Will! I almost hit the trees."

No attacker! Relief rose in Will, followed by shame for not acknowledging that she could have died from the impact. He moved closer and laid a gentle hand on her back, directing her to the couch. "It's okay, Sybil. You're okay now."

He blinked when he saw what was in her eyes. Not fear; more like—wonder?

"I felt it, Will. Really felt it," she hiccuped as fresh tears slid down her cheeks.

Confused, he gave a slight shake of his head and waited.

"The baby—our baby. It fluttered, like a butterfly, moving across my insides. Oh, Will! It happened when I sat in the truck trying to get the nerve to back out onto the road. That's when I felt it." She looked down at where her hand had migrated to the spot just below her waist.

The impact of her words hit him fuzzy at first, then with bright clarity, like fog lifting on a spring day. *It's true. She's pregnant.* Will dismissed his anger and hurt. He moved closer, ready to pull her into an embrace.

"Oh, Will, this time I don't want to—" Sybil clamped a fist over her mouth, her eyes round.

"Shh. You won't lose this one, sweetheart. I promise. We'll see Doc as soon as possible, maybe tomorrow. I'll make him see you, no matter how busy he is. And you won't have to lift a finger this time." He pulled her into the embrace. "I won't let it happen again."

Sybil laid her head on Will's shoulder. She spoke barely above a whisper. "Before, it was like the baby was far away. Like it had a long journey and wouldn't arrive for a long time. But now I know it's here with us. Think of it. It's in this room at this very moment. That's something, isn't it, Will?"

A new thought for him, too. Not sure how to reply, he pulled her even closer, but she stiffened and wiggled loose. Baffled by the sudden change, he looked to her face. But she'd already turned away and started for the staircase.

"I'm tired now, Will. I just want to rest."

"Of course. I'll help you upstairs, then I'll call Doc," he said as he fell into step beside her.

Back downstairs, Will called Doctor Jennings and made arrangements. As he hung up he spotted Sybil's purse where she'd dropped it when she entered the house. A seed of doubt shot through him. He stared at the purse for a long moment, then grabbed it and rummaged through the contents. Five one-dollar bills lay crumpled on the bottom. He felt his own flutter then, as the familiar feeling of disappointment and anger returned.

Chapter 9

*T*he boat pushed against the strong current of the swollen river. Tilly watched Josiah's back muscles bulge with each row, straining to pull the oars through the rolling water. Her own muscles ached from the weight of the act she'd committed three weeks ago when she'd given Josiah ground mustard leaves in a bottle labeled *Cohosh*.

"Tell her to make a tea of the leaves, just like the other times."

Now she'd told another lie to Josiah for him to pass on to the wife of the man who made the three small crosses. Her mind recalled a lie she'd told Big Mama when she was a young girl.

"You stay outa the berry patch, child. They's too green to eat yet. Don't bring nothin' but belly trouble if you eat them afore they ripe," Big Mama instructed, her hands on her hips.

The desire for the berries came too strong, and

that night, when stomach pains began, Big Mama guessed the cause. "Tilly, you eat them berries after I done told you not to?"

She saw the hurt in her grandmother's eyes when the response was an emphatic, "No, ma'am."

Big Mama stood over her, quiet for a moment; then she spoke in a whisper. "I cain't make you tell the truth, child. But always remember, God knows what's in the heart of all His children. I reckon it's Him that's got to do the correctin'."

More than her stomach hurt now. Every muscle in her body ached with a shame. *I'm surely weary of livin' a lie. Now I'm lying to my customers and even to my friend Josiah.*

As they often did, Big Mama's words came loud and clear. "Life will make its way back to you, Tilly."

"I give up on that a long time ago, Big Mama." Tilly fussed, in the habit of talking to Big Mama as if her grandmother were standing next to her. "You shouldn't'a put such a foolish idea in a young girl's head. Reckon I know what life is now, and it ain't got nothin' to do with the hope you talked 'bout back then."

Josiah's boat made the bend and moved out of sight. She forced her mind back to her task for the day: the small cluster of mayapple plants growing in the thickest part of the forest. A short walk north of the river and Tilly was soon picking the green mayapples.

Bent from the waist, she pulled the unripe fruit with both hands, dumping handfuls into her basket. Waiting for the fruit to ripen on the plant meant possibly losing it to animals drawn by its sweet smell. Back home, she would bury the fruit in dried-out used coffee grounds until they turned a golden yellow, perfect for making sweet jam.

Her hands moved in swift motion while her feet took slow steps, moving past one plant to the next effortlessly. It left her mind open to play the events of Josiah's visit over and over, like a movie reel.

"I cain't be givin' customers the wrong stuff. Anybody finds out, nobody'll ever buy from me again. I gotta get them crosses outa my mind." She pulled so hard at a cluster of mayapples her feet stumbled. Immediately, she was on the ground, crushing the plants she'd just picked from. Frustration sparked as her eyes swelled with tears. *What be the matter with me today? Why'm I so unsettled?*

Upright, she turned to the flattened plants and yanked several stalks out of the ground, exposing a long taproot. After they dried, she'd grind the roots to make a compound perfect for removing warts and other skin growths.

Her back ached from bending over to search under the large umbrella-shaped leaves of the knee-high plants. Satisfied with a full basket of mayapples, she yanked at the burlap sack which held the stalks pulled from the moist, soft ground.

She never left the cabin without the basket and the sack. They gave her the ability to carry what she forged from the forest and left her arms free to work. When she first started foraging she hauled only a large basket, but found it too clumsy. The small basket and sack attached to her waist became her daily uniform. Inside the sack, she carried a pick and a small knife to aid in her work—and as potential weapons.

Finished and ready for a rest, Tilly walked toward

the hives and crouched behind a large tree to scan the open meadow for the beekeeper. With no one about, she moved to rest in the shade of a large spruce. The buzzing from the hives usually soothed her agitated soul as she lay in the soft grass with her eyes closed.

Not today. She kept opening her eyes to survey her surroundings, unable to relax. Then a shiny object sitting on a fallen log caught her attention. She crept closer until she could make out a jar filled with honey. Thoughts swirled like the bees around their hives.

Is it for me? Did he see me when I foolishly laughed? Is it a trap, to lure me outa the woods?

Her heart raced hard. She fell to her knees to lessen the space the blood had to flow. After several moments, she raised up and looked about.

Is somebody here now? Is they waitin' for me to take the jar just so's they can grab me up? Part of her thought this would be okay. No more loneliness, no more forging to survive, no more men's clothing. But in her mind's eye, she saw the past. *Best stay with what I know. Got to be better than the unknown.*

She rose slowly and turned back toward the dark forest, stepping carefully on the forest floor to avoid small twigs which packed a loud crack if broken by her boots. Tilly willed her mind to think about the forest, but thoughts of the honey returned.

She could taste the sweet, strong taste as if licking it off her finger. Desire grew greater than fear. She spun around and headed back to the hives. "I'll wait 'til dark, grab it, and zig-zag home so's I cain't be followed."

Tilly stared at the red-checked cloth covering the jar from where she sat at her table. As soon as she returned from the beehives last evening, she'd shoved the jar to the back of her food shelf and covered it with the cloth. Falling into her bed, she fell into a fitful sleep, more awake than asleep. Each time her eyes opened, they surveyed the cabin and landed on the jar that sat in the moonlight shining through the window. It had become an enemy, yet it pulled at her, beckoning her to open it and taste the sweet nectar.

The sun had just appeared when she took the jar from under the cloth and grabbed a plate, a spoon, and some cornbread from the tin. After spreading a generous amount of honey on her plate, she used what remained on the spoon to drizzle some on a piece of silt grass for Solomon.

"Come on, you might as well be my partner in crime," Tilly said and watched Solomon crawl slowly toward the bit of grass.

She sopped big hunks of cornbread into the plate of honey, allowing the sticky liquid to run down her forearm and beyond the plate. Finished, she surveyed the messy table. "Well, Solomon, I don't know about you, but I sure enjoyed that."

The smile left as quickly as it came. She grabbed the lid, secured it on the jar, and returned it to the food shelf. Not satisfied, she snatched it back and searched her cabin for a better hiding place. Crossing the cabin to the bed, Tilly knelt and pushed the jar as far as she could reach under the bed. She stood, walked to the door, and surveyed the cabin.

Still too close!

Tilly rushed outside with the jar and cloth

tucked in the crook of her arm. She threw open the cellar door and scrambled down the steps. Waiting a moment to adjust to the darkness, she moved to the far corner. There, long ago, she'd dug a hole in the soft dirt and lined it with tree bark. A place for the letters Big Mama had written before she passed.

Near the river, a safe distance from the cabin, Tilly and her grandmother sometimes communicated through letters left in the deep hollows of a fallen log. She tore into each letter the moment she retrieved it, then ignored Big Mama's warning, "Burn these letters after you read them, child." After her grandmother died, she often pulled them from the hole and read the words while she swiped at tears caused by the familiar writing.

Tilly pushed the letters to one side and shoved the jar next to them. She covered all the items with the red cloth and replaced the wooden potato box in front of the hole. Calmness followed, and she returned to the cabin to wash off the honey and dirt.

Scrubbing until her hands and forearms burned from the rough cloth and lye soap, she realized the wetness on her face were tears.

Even a simple jar of honey became her enemy.

Chapter 10

A sweat ring formed around the band of Will's hat, threating to run down his forehead and into his eyes. The blistering mid-morning August sun promised an even hotter afternoon. He moved the bushel basket of peas into the shade of his roadside stand, hoping they would sell before the day was over. Otherwise, he'd be spending his evening shelling and canning them.

He'd opened the stand several years back to sell his apples and produce. Travelers on the county road often stopped at the roadside stand near the turn to his orchard to purchase apples or fresh garden vegetables.

He glanced at his tomatoes, placed in luscious red rows on the rough wooden table. The temptation too great, he grabbed one, wiped the sand off with his palms, and sunk his teeth into the soft, rich insides.

When a new Hudson came to a stop in front of his stand, Will swiped the juices off his chin and tossed the remains into the grass. He smiled widely. From the looks of the car, this person might pay more than what he was asking of others. He debated whether it would be wrong to push up the cost of whatever they bought.

At the sight of Eleanor Rhode exiting the driver's side, his smile slide into a straight line. Could she know about the loan? Maybe Carl changed his mind? The sound of a window lowering from the passenger's side torn him from his thoughts.

"Hi, Mr. Will," Danny said as he leaned out the window.

"Hi there, Danny. I haven't seen you riding your horse for a while." He couldn't help but smile back at Danny's obvious happiness.

"Mama say, 'No Danny, too hot to ride. Wait.'" He grinned even while shaking his head from side to side. "I waiting, Mr. Will."

"The weather will change soon, Danny. It always does."

He turned to face Eleanor. "Hello, Mrs. Rhode. How are you?"

"Good morning. I didn't know you were selling vegetables."

"I am this year. With the baby coming soon, we can use the extra funds." He gulped, wishing he could take the words back. *Does she know about our money problems?* Trying again, words tumbled out of his mouth. "It'll be an apple stand again come October."

"Congratulations on the baby. When's it due?"

"October, same time as the apple crop comes in."

"Then you'll have a bumper crop this year."

"Yes, ma'am. I can't disagree with that." He

chastised himself for the ridiculous notions about why she was there. "What can I get for you today?

"I need tomatoes. Cut worms got to mine. I'd like all you have, please. I plan to do some canning. Are those purple hull peas?"

"Sure are, about the last for this year. Would you like them also?"

"Yes, and can you hold them for me until I come back from town? I'd hate for them to get hot in the car."

"Sure thing. I'll be out here until sunset today. Hope to clear out enough of the produce to make room for what needs picking in the morning."

"Thank you, Will. I'm sure we'll be back long before sunset. We're just going to the bank." She opened her purse to remove a five-dollar bill. "Is this enough?"

Will cringed inwardly. He struggled with an answer. It was twice what he'd normally charge. Yet... Carl Rhode could afford for his wife to drive a new Hudson, while Sybil drove his old truck.

"Yes, that'll do." He grabbed the bill and stuffed it into his overall pocket.

"Danny, say goodbye to Mr. Will."

"Bye, Mr. Will. We go to town now."

"Bye, Danny. See you later."

"Later!" Danny laughed, and rapidly waved his hand.

Will watched the car out of sight. It was only then he realized Eleanor never removed her sunshades. And why would anyone wear long sleeves in this unrelenting heat?

Eleanor drove at a slow speed so Danny could see the sights along the way to town. He chattered about the cows, the cornfields, and the few houses that sprinkled the route to Berkley. She responded each time with *hmm* or *oh, my*—enough to keep Danny engaged. But her mind roamed far from the scenery. She thought about recent conversations with her husband. Actually, more like demands. Lately, his talk had been full of "being responsible" and "making sure accounts áre in order."

Today, he'd insisted she come to town to sign some papers. She tried to talk him out of it, and the conversation escalated to an angry scene. Now she drove to town with puffy red eyes and bruised arms. Fear scaled its way through her body as a thought she'd tried to keep at bay emerged. He'd never before hurt her when he was sober.

Eleanor sped up for the last few miles to Berkley, eager to have done with what Carl demanded and return home. She looked forward to time in her kitchen canning tomatoes. Tomorrow morning, she'd sit on the front porch and shell the peas. Maybe she'd get Danny to help. She always enjoyed having her son near her.

At the square, she found a parking spot between the bank and the diner. The diner was Danny's favorite place. He'd sit in the corner booth where he could see both ways down Main Street and McDowell Street and give an enthusiastic wave to people who walked past his window.

Eleanor sometimes left him there under the watchful eye of Emma Grimes, her only friend though one she rarely saw outside of the diner. Carl wouldn't have approved, always pushing her to be friends with the women in the Berkley Ladies Society.

"They're in our class, Eleanor. The type of ladies you should be with."

But Eleanor never felt comfortable with the ladies. Their talk about new hair styles and favorite recipes always migrated to town gossip. She enjoyed Emma's company far more than the meetings and various teas and galas Society women held.

She smiled when she remembered what Emma said one day as they sat having coffee. "I'd rather wrestle a rattlesnake than go to one of those meetings. At least it warns you before it strikes!"

Eleanor loved how easy it was to be with Emma, a welcome respite from the times Carl expected her to "Act refined. Remember whose wife you are."

She and Danny walked into the diner, welcoming the air coming from the overhead fans. Emma worked at a table near the door, wiping it down for the next customer.

"Hello, Eleanor. Hi, Danny. Are you here for your Orange Crush?"

"Uh-huh. Mama say burger, too."

"Well, your favorite booth is empty, so you have a seat and I'll get your drink. Your burger will come out, quick as a wink."

"Quick as a wink, Emma!" Danny laughed, enjoying the game he and Emma always played.

"Can you keep an eye on him, Emma?" Eleanor asked. "I have to go to the bank and...well, you know how that goes."

"No problem, sweetheart. You know I love having Danny around." Emma laid a hand on her friend's arm. "I'm sorry you have to go into that stuffy old bank on such a hot day." She narrowed her eyes at Eleanor, scanning her clothing. "Although from the looks of those long sleeves, heat doesn't seem to bother you."

"Please, no lectures today, Emma. Whatever Carl wants will be hard enough," she whispered urgently.

Emma tipped her head and offered a soft smile. "Okay, honey, you go get your business over. Danny and I will be fine right here. And afterwards, we'll find an empty booth and enjoy a cup of coffee. But remember—you need to give back same as you get."

"Thank you, Emma." She turned to her son. "Danny, you be good for Emma. Enjoy your burger."

"Yes, Mama. You be good, too."

The lobby of the bank sweltered as the day's heat rose. Women politely waved small fans over their faces; men removed their hats often to wipe their brow. Bank employees looked sluggish as they worked with sweaty hands.

Eleanor walked straight to Carl's office, expecting to see his secretary at her desk outside his door. With no one about, Eleanor sat in one of the two chairs placed against the wall of his office. She knew better than to go in unannounced. The one time she did made Carl to fly into a temper about her unrefined ways.

Five minutes—then ten. Eleanor wondered if perhaps both had gone to an early lunch. Then she heard a loud giggle from inside the office. She jumped from her seat when the door opened and Molly Wagner walked out. Eleanor had never seen her unkempt, but now, strands of hair fell from the bun, her makeup smeared.

"Oh, Mrs. Rhode. How nice to see you. Hot day, ain't—uh, isn't it?" she squeaked, her voice louder than usual. "Mr. Rhode is just inside. We've been... uh... working on some files. Go right in."

Shame and anger warred within Eleanor. She started toward the door, then turned back. "Thank you, Miss Wagner. I know Carl appreciates your help. Filing can be such a tedious job. I'm sure you'd much rather be here in the lobby where there's not so much... hot air." She smiled sweetly at the secretary, who still worked feverishly to correct her hair style.

"Eleanor, good to see you! I'm glad you came in. I told Miss Wagner I'd like to take my wife to lunch." Carl spoke in a loud, overly friendly voice. "But I'm sure you feel as I do. It's too blasted hot to eat."

"Please, just tell me what it is you want me to do. I left Danny at the diner. I don't want to be too long," she said in a monotone voice, placing her purse on the edge of his desk.

"Well, that's just what I want to talk to you about. Our sons. You know, we're not getting any younger and Johnny was just in here the other day saying we should think about getting our affairs in order in case... well, you know."

"No, I don't know, Carl. Tell me what you need. As much as you and others seem to enjoy this hot, stuffy office, I don't. I'd like to finish this business and collect Danny." Her eyes pierced him with contempt.

Carl's smile slide from his face, replaced with the slightly pursed lips—a gesture she knew meant he was calculating his next move. He shuffled papers on his desk and pulled a thin blue folder from the stack. "It's simple, Eleanor. I have a revised copy of our will to make Johnny the sole heir. You need to sign in two places, and you'll be out of this hot office."

Eleanor's mouth dropped open. Her heart leaped, threatening to take her breath. "You can't do this, Carl. You have two sons. They're both your heirs." As soon as the words came from her mouth, she wished she could take them back. He never responded well to an order.

Three steps around the desk brought Carl close to her side. She could feel his breath on her neck. "Now you hear me on this, Eleanor. Danny wouldn't know if he had twelve cents or twelve thousand dollars. What's he going to do with an inheritance? Why, he'd probably give it to the first scam artist who came by. What I own, what I've worked for, will go to my oldest son." He grabbed her hand, squeezing so hard she let out a small groan. "Now, take the pen and sign the papers. Then forget about it. Let the man of the family handle this type of thing."

Barely able to see through her tears, Eleanor scratched her name on the two places Carl moved her hand to. Who would care for Danny when she died? Oh, how could she be so weak? *Forgive me, Danny.*

Outside the bank, Eleanor breathed in the air she'd lost in Carl's office. A slow walk to the diner gave her time to calm down. Never would she have taken anything from Danny—but she just denied him the inheritance a son should have. She thought of all the times she stood silent while Carl demeaned her, or worse. Each time she took it because it protected

Danny's future. Now, Carl had taken her son's inheritance with the few strokes of a pen.

She found Danny finishing a bowl of ice cream, compliments of Emma. Thankfully, her friend worked frantically to cover the lunch rush. All Emma could do was give her a quick wave.

Mouthing a quick thank you, Eleanor hustled Danny out of the diner and into the car. She wanted to be as far from Berkley and First Security Bank as possible.

Sales were good and by mid-afternoon only a few cucumbers and some green onions lay on the table. Will sat on an upturned crate as he watched for Eleanor, eager to close early. Leaving now meant time to pick some produce before sundown.

He heard Eleanor's car before he saw it. When it came into sight, he stood, prepared to load her purchase. The Hudson moved at a high speed and passed the vegetable stand.

Will watched it out of sight. Scratching his head, he debated what to do. If he took the tomatoes and peas to Eleanor's home, he might run into Carl. The thought made his blood chill. He'd had enough humiliation at the hands of that man.

Chapter 11

*D*ew sparkled on the garden when Will arrived to pick the vegetables ready to harvest. Daisy followed close by, sniffing the dirt to identify where rabbits had nibbled the night before.

"I'd be beholden, Daisy, if you'd make it a nightly chore to take care of the rabbits and other critters who think this garden is theirs."

The dog stopped long enough to give Will a look, then put her head back down and trotted off to follow a hot trail.

Will smiled. He enjoyed his dog, sometimes more than his wife. Images of scenes carried out over the summer swam through his head, threatening to drown him in misery. He tried so hard to make Sybil comfortable, to ease the trials of pregnancy. At first, she reveled in the idea of a baby. The memory of those first movements sustained her. But as the days grew hotter, and she grew bigger, she changed. Now she seemed interested only in her needs, not the baby.

Last night proved the worst. The steamy heat put both in cranky moods. Will arrived home from the produce stand to find Sybil madder than a wet hen.

"Will Parson, I've been waiting for you all afternoon. But do you drop by for even a moment? No! You'd rather be at your stupid produce stand, selling from the side of the road like a tenant farmer, than helping your pregnant wife. I've a mind to pack up and go home. At least I'd have someone to help me."

He'd heard the threat so many times, Will almost wished she'd do it. His patience wore thin; yet if she went home, she might never return. The threats stayed with him long into the night, robbing him of much-needed rest. Somehow, he had to make sure this didn't happen. But now, he had little restraint left. His temper rose as high as the late afternoon heat.

Will waited until she ran out of words, more from experience than patience. "All right, Sybil. I'm here now. I don't think it's good for you to get so upset. Why don't we go inside; I'll help you put your feet up. Then we can talk."

"I don't want to sit down. I've sat all day. I'm craving a burger from Ben's Diner. I want you to take me to town so I can have one."

Looking at his wife with her bottom lip in a pout lit a fuse in Will. In a low, determined voice, he responded, "Sybil, I've been in the sun since early this morning, and before that I picked vegetables to sell. The last thing I plan to do is drive to Berkley for a burger!" Will scooted past her. Inside, he turned and said in a softer voice, "Besides, you know we need to save money to pay the doctor when the baby comes. We'll have the rest of the stew I made yesterday."

"Oh, you...you awful man. Maybe I'll move back home with my parents. They'd get me a burger. I'm sick of you and this place—and I'm sick of this baby!"

A restless night spent on the small single bed in the spare room did little to ease the fear growing in him. Would Sybil carry out her threat? How could he manage the farm and keep her happy? Something else kept him awake in the long hours before daybreak, too: a sack of tomatoes and a bushel of peas.

Drizzling rain didn't improve his already foul mood. Picking vegetables would be wet work and chances were few customers would stop to buy produce in this weather.

Regardless, he had to keep the stand open. They needed the money. Besides, given a choice, Will preferred to be out in foul weather than in the dry house with a disagreeable wife.

Breakfast skipped, he downed a quick cup of coffee, then grabbed a rain slicker and headed for the garden. Daisy watched him from the porch, not willing to get wet. "Don't blame you, girl," Will said. "It's a soggy mess out here."

By the time he'd harvested the vegetables, the sun peeked through the clouds in the eastern sky. Hopeful the rain had ended, he picked up his pace and arrived at the stand just as the drizzle stopped.

Within minutes, Daisy came running to Will. "So, now you show up. Guess you really are a fair-weather friend," he said, pleased to have his companion at his side.

The morning moved slowly. As expected, sales were slow even though the sky remained blue and the produce shone from the fresh rain and gleaming sunlight. At noon, Will grabbed a slate and a piece of chalk to make a sign. *Back in 30 minutes. Help yourself. Leave the cash in the cigar box.*

He walked back to the house, grabbed the tomatoes and peas off the porch, and loaded them into his truck. His stomach, empty from a lack of breakfast and now with no noon meal, tightened and rolled to remind him of the void. He grimaced as the cramp moved from his left side to his gut, then fussed at himself for being nervous.

Why should I care what Carl Rhode thinks? It's not like we move in the same social circles. Heck, I don't even have a social circle! Once again, he thought of how little he had outside of his apples. With his mother gone and a discontented wife, he'd never felt more alone.

Then he thought of the baby who'd arrive in a few months. His child! A part of him—and an heir to the place he loved. His thoughts of a child pushed Carl Rhode to the smallest creases of his mind as insignificant. "I'll make it without his money. I'll do it for my child," he said as he turned into Eleanor's driveway. Still, he searched for Carl's vehicle, relieved not to see it.

Eleanor answered the door after the first ring. "Will, is everything okay? It's not Sybil's time, is it?

"No, nothing like that. I have the produce you bought yesterday. You forgot to stop back by on your way home. You already paid me, so I thought I ought to get them to you."

Eleanor's eyes filled with confusion, then clarity. "Oh, I'm so sorry. Why, I can't imagine how I could have forgotten the beautiful tomatoes and peas. Please forgive me. I've taken you away from your stand."

"No problem. Customers are typically good with the honor system. They take what they want and leave their money behind. I reckon we have honest folks in this county. Wouldn't you agr—"

"I'm glad you stopped. I need a favor, and you're the only person I think I can ask."

After his time in her husband's office, the last thing he wanted was more involvement with her family. Still, he could hear his mother's words about being a good neighbor.

"I'm happy to help if I can, Mrs. Rhode."

"Please call me Eleanor," she responded with a smile which instantly put Will at ease. "You attend Lick Creek Bible Church, right?"

"Well, yes, but it's really my mom's church. I've not attended much since she passed."

He didn't want to share how he'd given up trying to persuade Sybil to attend the church with him. In his mind, he could hear his wife saying, *Attend that pitiful little country church? Really, Will. They don't even have an organ. I'd much prefer to go to the Presbyterian church in town. All the best people go there.*

Will found it easier to stay home on Sunday mornings and catch up on his endless work list. He'd only be going because he knew it would've pleased his mom anyway. The more he struggled with his life, the less interested he was in God.

"But you know Pastor Gandy. Didn't you and he grow up together?"

He didn't want to tell Eleanor that he and Bill didn't exactly run in the same circles. As an athletic, Will often said and did things the son of a preacher would never do or say.

"Yes, I know him, but—"

"Then could you please help me meet him? I need someone I can talk. It's important to me." Will could see the pleading in her eyes.

He paused, then said, "Sure, I can arrange a meeting." Although how he'd set it up evaded him. Still, he knew he'd do most anything for this kind woman who seemed desperate.

"Another thing, Will." She paused, swallowed hard, and continued. "I'd like to see him without Carl knowing. He wouldn't understand, probably ask me why I didn't see Reverend Wheeler." Her words tumbled over each other as small beads of sweat formed on her forehead.

Intuitively, Will knew not to press. "I suppose I could ask him to come over one afternoon. You could visit with him at my place."

Relief flooded Eleanor's face. "I'll make some fresh bread for you and Sybil. I'm sure she must be struggling with this heat. Baking's always hard by seven months. If Brother Gandy were visiting when I came by, well, that would seem normal—right?"

Will thought it anything but right, but he smiled and nodded his head "Should be. I'll ask Brother

Gandy to come over Sunday afternoon around three." *But what on earth am I going to give as a reason?*

The bright look in Eleanor's eyes made him determined to find a way. Regardless of how he felt about church, he wanted to help her with whatever the problem might be.

"Guess I'd better get back to my stand. I'll see you around three on Sunday," he said with more confidence than he felt. *What if the pastor is busy or refuses to call on such a wayward member? No, I'll get him there, even if I have to bribe him with an offering to his church!*

"But I don't understand. Why is the pastor coming here? He hasn't been in this house since your mother died."

Will sighed, wishing Sybil would let it drop. But since he told her about Brother Gandy's visit, she'd questioned him nonstop about the reason for the visit. Her latest almost brought a chuckle from Will. *I guess it's too much to let a pregnant woman get her afternoon nap. Now I'm forced to entertain a country preacher.* When had anything stopped his wife from a nap?

Will stuck to his guns and assured her there'd be no need to entertain. It would be a brief visit, often done on Sunday afternoons. He hoped she would just nap through it, especially when Eleanor came to the door unannounced.

Sunday morning, Will left the house at daylight, a cup of coffee in his hand and Daisy at his heels. He intended to keep busy outside until noon, then he'd have time to clean the house before Brother Grandy and Eleanor arrived. Doubts flooded his mind when he thought about what could happen if Carl found out his part in Eleanor's deception. More than once, he wished he'd never agreed to this.

He didn't look forward to what the preacher might question him about, either. Although Will had to admit, the man had been very cordial about coming over. He'd given a loose reason about how they were expecting a child soon and would like to have a dedication ceremony shortly after the baby's birth. Not exactly a lie since he knew his mother would want it. He'd decided not to push his issues with God onto his child—it could decide for itself.

In a few hours, his part would over, and he'd be glad for it. Although how he'd answer Sybil's questions still escaped him.

He stepped onto the porch when the sun stood overhead, surprised to hear the broom swishing across the rug in the parlor. Inside, he froze when he saw his wife sweeping.

"Wipe your feet, Will Parson. I've been cleaning all morning. The last thing I want is for a man of the cloth to find my house dirty," Sybil said, never looking up from the spot she swept.

Will's mouth dropped open. *My house?* His wife never referred to it as her house—only as a drafty old farmhouse. Hope began as a small droplet and grew as he watched Sybil attacking the floor as if it were her mortal enemy. *Has she finally accepted this place?* Did it only take visitor for his wife to take ownership of their home?

At his silence, Sybil turned around and barked,

"Don't just stand there until you take root. Get over here and finish this sweeping. My back hurts, my feet are swollen as big as melons, and I want something to eat." She let the broom handle fall to the floor as she waddled off to the kitchen.

Hope flowed out of Will like water through a sieve. Each time she made him hopeful she had found happiness with their life, the old Sybil showed up within moments. He chastised himself for thinking she had changed.

Brother Gandy knocked on the door at three sharp, as promised. Sybil had disappeared in their bedroom a couple hours earlier. Will hoped she'd decided to nap. But as soon as a knock came from the door, she came down the stairs dressed in a fresh skirt and maternity top, her hair and makeup done.

"Will!" she hissed. "Don't just stand there gawking at me like you've never seen me before. Let the man in."

For the next ten minutes, Sybil played the perfect hostess, offering their guest some iced tea and small cakes that she'd recently hoarded for herself. Will stared at the scene before his eyes. Could this charming lady be his wife? He'd not offered much more than a nod to the conversation.

Another knock at the door made Sybil swing her eyes at her husband. "Why, who could that be? You didn't mention anyone else dropping by." Her eyes bore into Will's before she looked back at the preacher. "Excuse me, please. I must see to the door," she said, with the air of a proper lady.

Sybil rose as Will shot out of his chair. "No, I'll get it, Sybil. Stay where you are."

"Why, thank you, dear. You're always so considerate of me. As I said, Reverend Gandy..."

"Please, call me Brother Bill," the pastor said as his eyes and Sybil's moved to the door of the parlor, where Eleanor stood with a loaf of bread.

"I'm so sorry to disturb you and your rest, Sybil. I've brought you fresh bread. I know how hard it must be to bake in heat like this."

"Oh, this so neighborly of you, Eleanor. I'll just take it to the kitchen." Sybil stood and crossed over to Eleanor, reaching for the loaf. "I'll be right back. Would you like a glass of iced tea? I'm sure you're parched after driving over."

Again, Will stared at his wife. *Is this the same person who has done nothing but complain for the past four months?*

He turned back to the preacher. "Brother Bill, I wonder if you could give Eleanor some of your time. I'm sure you'll find the porch comfortable for visiting." He held his breath, hopeful there'd be no questions— questions to which he had no answers.

"I'd be happy to." He motioned for Eleanor to walk through the door before him, with only a slight questioning glance at Will as he passed. Admiration for the grace of this pastor flooded Will.

He stood alone in the parlor when Sybil returned with a glass of tea.

"Where'd they go? I have Eleanor's iced tea." She looked at Will, her forehead wrinkled with confusion.

"They're on the porch."

"Well, for goodness' sake. Why are they out there

in this heat? I'll get them back inside." She started for the door when Will reached out and squeezed her arm.

"Sybil Parson, you stay away from the door," he said in a low growl. "They're in a private conversation and I'll not allow you to interrupt them." For once, his wife didn't demand her way and retreated to the sofa.

Chapter 12

*T*he coffee sat cold on the wicker table next to
Eleanor. She'd brought her coffee to the massive
front porch to sit on one of the white wicker rockers.
She hoped for some quiet time before Danny got up,
clamoring for his pancakes, and asking, as he did every
morning, to "help flip 'em." She smiled at the thought
of their morning ritual, which always brightened her
day, even when troubles seemed to hang over her like
dark clouds.

The early morning sun rose from behind the
mountain in front of the house. As the first light made
its assent, the tops of the trees, which wore their fall
foliage of red, yellow, and orange, took on a golden hue.
Eleanor sat still, an audience of one, and observed the
spectacle as the sun bathed the trees in light, moving
from their tops and down to their trunks.

As she watched, Eleanor thought of a phrase her
mother shared with her the night she and Carl told

her parents they'd eloped. Her father hugged her and shook hands with Carl, seeming pleased his daughter would have a life he could never give his family.

What her mother said pierced her heart. She hugged Eleanor, then stepped back to stare at her daughter's face with eyes full of great sadness which never went away. Not since her oldest son, Patrick, had died in the Battle of Verdun in The Great War and her next son, Sean, died in a mining accident. Now her youngest son, Rudy, spoke of nothing expect when he would be old enough to be a miner. She stared into Eleanor's hopeful blue eyes and whispered, "Remember, daughter, all that glitters isn't gold."

How true. She'd learned possessions meant little. Her entire marriage, she'd yearned for the love she'd grown up with in her family, a love that protected and cherished, built on an unbreakable bond of oneness. Certainly not one of humiliation and hurt.

With a quiet sigh, Eleanor's mind moved back to when she first met Carl. She often spent her afternoons at the Claymore Mine Company school that the children of miners attended. She herself had gone to school there and had many fond memories of days spent reading books from the classroom library. She loved to help students who struggled with reading. The teacher welcomed her assistance.

Snow fell the day the principal entered the classroom asking for everyone's attention. Next to him stood a handsome man in his late twenties dressed in a dapper pin-striped suit, his Gatsby bowler hat covered with snow.

His eyes roved the classroom as the principal said, "Mr. Rhode is the temporary mine superintendent until a new one arrives at the end of the summer." He looked at Carl as he waited for him to say a few words to the students. At that moment, Carl's eyes fell on Eleanor and there they stayed.

"I'm happy to be here, children, especially after seeing all the beauty here."

Eleanor blushed, knowing the intent of the pro tem superintendent's statement. A girlish pride in being noticed by a handsome man soon replaced her indignation. A few weeks later, Carl Rhode told her he'd decided in that moment to marry this lovely coal miner's daughter.

For the next six months, he romanced Eleanor with all the care and restraint of a true gentleman. Carl filled her head with the greatness of his plantation home and the fact that one day, when he finished his time at the mine learning how to operate a business, he would return to Berkley and take his father's place at the bank.

She shook her head at how gullible she'd been. She wanted to marry someone who wasn't a miner. Someone who could care for her and give her children a future beyond mining.

She ignored the plentiful signs, such as the time spent with her instead of in the mine office and the faint smell of liquor when they sat together in the swing on her parent's small front porch. She even ignored the subtle remarks of disdain about the miners. All she saw was a way out, and she fantasized Carl to be the one she had dreamed of since a young girl—her knight in shining armor.

Brother Franks' words from the night before came to her as clearly as if he were sitting in the rocker next to her. He spoke of her being a daughter of the king and the eternal inheritance God offers to those who believe. That came after she spilled her fear and frustration at her husband's plan to leave his estate to only one son, Johnny. She'd expected a man of God to agree with her it would be a wrongful act. Yet he'd only smiled and talked to her about a heavenly inheritance.

"As a child of God, Eleanor, you have an inheritance far greater than anything here on earth, and no man can take that from you."

She did believe that, even though in her marriage she often felt far from the God of her childhood. Growing up in a small mining town on the Gauley River, she attended a Baptist church every Sunday. At age thirteen, she'd accepted Christ's gift of salvation. She loved church and felt herself growing in her faith through her teenage years.

Since moving to Berkley, she attended the Presbyterian church with Carl—a church so different from the one back home, they might as well be on different planets. She lost her yearning for the word of God, as well as the peace that comes when one rests in him. She wanted it back, and Brother Frank helped her see God hadn't turned his back on her.

"You've turned from him, Eleanor. You only need to come back. He's there waiting for you with open arms." Brother Bill's words, spoken with such gentleness and compassion, hit their mark. Eleanor had asked God to forgive her for straying and to help her with the burdens she carried.

"I can't promise you that what has caused those dark rings under your eyes will go away. But I can promise you that God will be there with you," Brother Bill said after praying with Eleanor.

Now, alone on the porch in the crisp fall morning light, she prayed as she'd never prayed before. She asked God to take the resentment which lived beneath the surface of her every moment and to fill her with his mercy and grace. Then she prayed for Carl, asking God to give him a love for her and both his sons. As she prayed for her husband, a peace she'd not felt for years settled over her. Next, she prayed for Johnny and Danny. The prayer was long and heartfelt, spoken in the soft whisper.

When she lifted her head and opened her eyes, Johnny stood just outside the front door, staring at her. "Oh, good morning, son. Have you been there long?"

"Long enough to know you're praying. Hope you get whatever you asked the big man for."

"Thank you. I'm sure I will." She cringed at his callousness and measured her words with care, since her oldest son often took things she or Danny said to Carl. "Why are you up so early?"

"I'm headed to Charleston. I'm working on a sweet business deal. If all goes well, I'll be set for life. See you in a few days, Mother." He bounded down the steps toward his little roadster. "Maybe I'll bring home something nice for Danny-boy."

Eleanor knew there would be nothing for Danny when his brother returned. How often had he told his little brother he'd bring him something, only to come home empty-handed? Yet Danny always forgave his brother, whom he adored. His unconditional love for others amazed Eleanor. Could she learn to do the same?

"Is that Johnny racing down the drive?" Carl asked as he stepped out the front door.

Surprised he would ask her anything, she responded, "Yes; he said he was going to Charleston. Something about a business deal."

"That's my son—a sharp businessman like his dad." Carl stood with his hands on his hips, chest thrust outward.

She suppressed a giggle, thinking he looked like a rooster. "Yes, both our sons are intelligent, Carl."

"Well, I wouldn't go that far. Danny couldn't find his way out of a paper bag."

She worked hard to hold anger at bay. Hadn't she just prayed about this? "Maybe if you spent more time with Danny, you'd see how bright he can be."

"Time's precious, Eleanor. Especially for a man of my status. I can't afford to waste it. I've got a breakfast meeting now and a hunting club meeting after work. I won't be home for dinner."

She watched his back as he hurried to his car, the limp in his bad leg worse in the early morning chill.

I wonder what kind of hunting he plans to do.

Chapter 13

*L*ate October brought a riot of color along the road to Berkley. Will took his time, enjoying the majestic splashes of red, yellow, and orange. He didn't want to jostle the baskets of apples in the back of the truck. They were the last of the harvesting season, McIntosh and Jonathon apples whose colors matched the fall trees.

He'd given himself plenty of time to make it to the far side of town, where Lenny Demarco waited to load his large market truck with apples from the orchards in the county. Will liked Lenny, with his deep gravelly voice, ever-present smile, and a belly that jiggled with his contagious laugh. He always enjoyed the Demarco home, alive with action from six kids and two sets of grandparents, all under one roof. With no siblings and few relatives, Will soaked in the happy chaos. Today, he wanted to be the first at Lenny's in case the other farmers had more apples than the Demarco truck could haul.

If he couldn't get all his apples on Lenny's truck, he'd have to travel on to Lewisville, a trip which would keep him away from home longer than he wanted. Sybil saw Dr. Benson yesterday, and he said the baby could come anytime now. Will smiled at the thought of seeing his son or daughter. He wondered often which it might be—not that it mattered.

It had been a long few months. At first Sybil talked about the baby—always as a girl—but now she talked only of her discomfort and her wish it would all be over. It relieved him to have the harvest over. Maybe if he spent more time with Sybil, she'd get excited about the child. Now, she glared at him for long moments as if it was all his fault.

Even at a slower pace, Will arrived in Berkley too early to meet Lenny. He stopped at Ben's Diner for a cup of coffee, choosing to sit on a stool at the counter since the tables were full, in the middle of the breakfast rush.

"Hello, Will. I haven't seen you around for a while," Emma said, smiling at him as she did all the customers.

Will nodded to his best friend's wife, thinking again about how well-suited she was for serving others. She never hurried with a customer, no matter how busy she might be—unlike the diner's owner, an ex-army sergeant and as gruff as they come.

Ben cooked in the back kitchen and rarely come forward unless Emma needed help. His rough, "What do you want?" forced many patrons to order quickly, not wanting to be the cause of more grumpiness.

He came from the back now and headed to the coffeepot. "Will," he said with a slight nod of his head.

"Ben," Will responded.

"You got apples today?"

"Sure do, the last of the season. I'm headed to Lenny's to send them to market." Will didn't say more. Ben wasn't one for chitchat.

"If you don't sell them all, come back by before you leave town. I might want a few dozen to make some apple pies for the diner."

"I'll do that, Ben. Should finish in a couple hours if I don't have to drive to Lewisville. I'm hoping Lenny can take them all."

Ben nodded as he took a long swig of coffee, then he disappeared to the back.

A sudden hush in the diner made Will turn from the counter. Every diner watched through the windows at something happening at the bank. An agitated group of people had gathered. More joined them each moment, many of whom yelled and waved their arms.

Within minutes, a young man rushed into the diner and announced, "It's a run on the bank. The stock market crashed!"

Disbelief and fear swelled like a gigantic ocean wave and hit Will's gut. He'd deposited all his earnings from this year's apple harvest, and from his honey and produce sales, in the bank just last week.

He threw a nickel for his untouched coffee on the counter and bounded out of the diner. He had to get his apples on Lenny's truck.

His fear grew greater when he saw three farmers with their apples still loaded in the back of their trucks talking to Lenny's wife. Nausea swept over him when he realized Lenny's truck was not there.

The tires on the old truck spun as he pushed the gear stick into park without slowing down. He jumped from his seat and left the truck running. "What's going on? Where's Lenny?"

The farmers let Lenny's wife do the talking. "He left, Will. He had the first customer's apples on the truck when he heard about the run on the bank. Every penny we've got is in that bank. If we can't get it out, how will we live? He couldn't wait for the rest of you. He needs to get the apple money before there's no longer a market for them. I'm sure sorry, Will."

She twisted her apron with her hands. Two youngsters hung on her legs while other children stood around in a tight circle. Tears poured down her cheeks. "How are we gonna feed these babies if my Lenny can't sell the apples?"

Not waiting to hear more, Will bounded back to his truck and pulled onto the highway leading to Lewisville. *If I get there soon enough, maybe I can sell my produce to the distributor there. Maybe the banks there haven't closed yet.* He drove fast—better to sell bruised apples than none at all.

The needle on the gas gauge moved dangerously close to empty before Will arrived back in Berkley. He pulled into McAfee's gas station shortly before closing time. "Just twenty-five cent's worth, Jode," he said through his open window.

"Twenty-five cents won't get you far down the road," Jode responded in his slow, drawling speech.

Jode had been in school with Will from first grade through eighth grade, when he'd quit to help his ailing father with the gas station. Will knew him to be a good businessman, a good husband, and a good father. Someone he'd like to spend more time with, if only he had some time.

"Just going on by the bank, then home."

"You can save yourself a stop. The bank closed before noon today. Only a few customers got their money out before the doors locked and a closed sign went up in the window." Jode said it as calmly as if he were talking about yesterday's weather.

"You mean there wasn't enough money to cover the accounts?" Will hadn't thought the day could get worse, but it just did.

"Yep. Word is, Carl Rhode left through the back door. Whole town's upset. Some mighty nasty rumors going 'round." Jode placed the hose back on the pump, then turned to screw the lid on the truck's gas tank. He paused at Will's window, and continued, "I always thought my pockets were deeper than Carl's. Took my money out a few years back."

Will had no response. Now he was the one with empty pockets. *Maybe Jode is smarter than all of them.* He fished a quarter from his overalls to pay for the gas.

"Wait a minute, Will. I see some good-looking apples back there. I sure would like some applesauce with my morning biscuits. Don't suppose you could spare a bushel? We'll call it even on the gas."

Jode's wife's family had several apple trees. This man didn't need his apples. Still, Will appreciated the gesture. "Take any bushel you want, Jode."

When the diner came into sight on his way out of town, Will remembered Ben's earlier request to buy some apples. He grimaced at the time on his wristwatch. He needed to be home, but he couldn't pass the chance to sell more apples. The trip to Lewisburg had been a bust. News of the crash had already reached the apple distributors. He'd returned with every one of his apples. Will tried not to think of the money he still owed the last of his pickers or his last feed store bill—not to mention money for the doctor for the delivery of the baby.

He pulled into the only parking spot available at the diner, surprised at how busy the place was at four o'clock in the afternoon. Inside, he saw several familiar faces, most of them coal mine workers and farmers. They ingested the happenings of the day with strong cups of coffee. Everyone stopped their conversations when Will entered, as if he might bring better news than what they were discussing.

He gave the room a general nod, then spotted Emma behind the counter. "Ben around?"

"Ben, Will's back. I expect he's got those apples you wanted," Emma yelled through the opening between the kitchen and the diner.

"How many did you bring back, Will?" Ben asked when he emerged from the back.

"Oh, most of them. Actually, all of them," he responded in a low voice.

"I'll take two bushels." Ben hit the open key on the cash register and removed some coins to hand Will.

"Wait, this morning you only wanted enough to make a few pies," he stammered.

"Are you trying to tell me what to serve at my diner?" Ben glared at him.

"No, sir. I'll bring them in." Will spun around toward the front door.

"Wait a minute." Emma stopped him as he was leaving. "I'd love to make Jim some applesauce. I'll take a bushel, too, please."

"Are you sure, Emma?" he asked. He knew money was always tight for her family, even though Emma worked full time and Jim worked in the coal mines.

"You know Jim as well as I do. And you know he's a bear if he doesn't get his morning biscuits with applesauce. Homemade is much better than store brought."

Yes, he knew Jim well—they'd been best friends since grade school. And he never saw Jim grumpy about anything. Still, he could tell by Emma's voice not to argue with her. He gave her a nod and started out the door.

"Will, if you have some extra, I'd like a bushel. I've got a deep cellar. Be nice to have apples all winter," said Homer Cochrane as he pulled a worn wallet from his work pants.

Homer had just got his bossin' papers and worked as Fire Boss on the night shift; but still, he had a house full of kids and cared for his wife's elderly parents. Humbled by Homer's generosity, Will smiled in agreement.

"How about getting me a half bushel, Will?"

"I'll be takin' the other half."

Soon, everyone in the diner had requested a half or a full bushel of apples. Unable to speak, Will went to his truck and began unloading the apples. He'd still have half the load to return home, but thanks to those in his hometown, he'd at least be able to pay the last of his pickers. What he would do with the rest of his debts escaped him.

On the drive home, Will thought of things he could sell to pay the bills which lay open on his dining room table.

When he turned into his drive, Daisy didn't meet him. She always came running to the truck as soon as he turned into his place. Concerned, he looked around. As soon as he opened the truck door, he heard a loud, piercing scream from inside the house. He leaped from the truck and raced inside.

Chapter 14

Silence followed the piercing scream. Will wasn't sure which terrified him more, the silence or the scream. He took the porch steps two at a time and raced into the house. Inside, Daisy stood on the landing at the top of the staircase, barking frantically as she spun in circles.

"I'm coming, girl," he said as he bounded up the stairs.

The dog ran into the bedroom before him and placed her paw on the bed. She turned her head to him and let out a whine in response to Sybil's soft moans.

Will moved to the other side of the bed. "Sybil, talk to me, sweetheart. Tell me what to do."

When she looked at him with glazed eyes, urgency welled up in him. "I'm going to call Eleanor and Dr. Jennings. I'll be back as soon as I can. Daisy, stay with her."

No reply came from Sybil, but Daisy lifted her

other paw to the bed and laid down her head. If he was ever grateful for his faithful dog, it was then.

He raced down the stairs, grabbed the phone, and dialed zero for the operator. Immediately, he heard, "One moment, please."

"No, I can't wait. This is an emergency. Connect me with Eleanor Rhode," Will screamed into the phone's receiver while holding the candle-shaped base with a death grip.

"Ringing the number now, sir," the nasally voice replied.

He waited through four rings when the voice returned. "I'm sorry, sir. There's no answer at this number."

Will's mouth went dry. Unable to speak, he hung up. He stood to clear his head, when he remembered seeing Danny and Eleanor at the horse stables as he passed by earlier. He calculated how long it would take to drive to Eleanor's and back. Longer than he should be away. Yet the thought of having no help when the baby arrived filled him with terror. He dashed to his truck, determined to find Eleanor.

A light in the apple house stopped him in his tracks. *Did Juan forget to turn off the lights or is he still cleaning up?*

He ran to the door, pushed hard against it, and all but fell inside. His foreman spun around from the shelves where he worked at stacking apple baskets until the next harvest. "Señor, what's wrong?"

"Sybil's in labor. I hate to leave her, but I need to get help. Can you go to the Rhode home and ask Eleanor to come? No one is answering their phone, so check the stables. If Eleanor isn't there, go to the house. She may be back inside by then."

"Sí, I'll go fetch her." Juan grabbed his battered cowboy hat and started for the door. Almost there, he turned to Will. "Don't worry, Señor Parson. My Maria has had seven little ones now. These women, they have a way of making it happen."

Will wished he had the same confidence. More than anything, he wished his mom were there.

Another scream from the house brought him to the bedroom at a full run. Will tried to comfort Sybil as she thrashed about on the bed, but she never acknowledged his presence. She seemed to be in her own world—one full of demons.

He moved from her bedside to the window, hoping to see Eleanor's car coming down the drive. Another scream and he rushed to his wife's side. She latched on to his arm with a grip that stunned him. Even after the scream subsided, she held on tight.

"Will, I'm here."

He jerked at the sound of Eleanor's voice and spoke in a panicked whisper. "Thank goodness you're here! Something must be wrong. She's in a bad way."

Eleanor reached for Sybil's hand and withdrew it from his forearm, then cradled it in her own. She stared at Sybil for a moment before she asked, "When will Dr. Jennings be here?"

Will's eyes widened. "I didn't..."

"You haven't called him? Listen to me. Go downstairs and call now. Do that first. Do you understand?"

He nodded, struggling to keep his eyes on

Eleanor. They were pulled back to Sybil when her moaning became louder.

"Look at me," Eleanor demanded. "After you've talked to Dr. Jennings, start some water boiling. When it's boiled, bring it and the birthing kit back. I helped Sybil put the kit together last week. It's in the cabinet over the stove.

"Boiled water, birthing kit."

"But call the doctor first. That's important."

"Right, doctor first," he mumbled.

"And Will...you should pray. We might have to deliver this baby ourselves."

He drew a long breath to keep from hyperventilating. Praying wasn't something he'd done much of since his mother died. Why would God hear him now? No, he'd call the doctor. And if he had to, he'd help deliver his child. God hadn't shown up much in his life lately, so he didn't expect him to help today.

After a frustrating five-minute wait for the doctor's wife to get her husband to the phone, Will demanded he come immediately.

"Slow down there, Parson. How far apart are her pains?"

"There are no pains, just moaning. It's like she doesn't even know I'm there."

Dr. Jennings sighed. "Okay, I'm on my way. Do you have someone with you?"

"Eleanor Rhode is here. She's with Sybil now."

"Good, she's the one I'd want for this situation. Now, this is important, so hear me. Don't let your wife push until I arrive."

"Right, no pushing," Will repeated, terrified at the thought of why. "When will you get here?"

"Son, I can't get there until I get off the phone with you. Just listen to everything Eleanor says. She may need you if I don't arrive in time."

Don't arrive in time? Sweat poured down Will's back as fear clawed at his guts. No, his wife needed him, and so did his child. He took two deep breaths and rushed to the kitchen. "Boiled water, birthing kit, no pushing," became his mantra.

Lyddie Anne Parson arrived just minutes after he returned to the bedroom with the things Eleanor needed. It happened so quick he had no time to think, only to respond to the commands from Eleanor. Two screams from Sybil and his daughter slid into the world. Eleanor, totally in charge, cut the cord and wrapped the baby girl tightly in a blanket before handing her to her father.

"Will, listen to me. We're not finished yet. There's still work to be done." Eleanor's tone pulled his attention away from the bundle he held. "Take the baby downstairs to the kitchen. Heat water enough to get the chill off it, then carefully submerge her into the bath. Make sure you support her head. That's important. Give her a good cleaning, diaper her, and wrap her in a clean blanket." She paused to make sure Will was listening. "Don't let her stay unwrapped very long. You need to keep her warm. While you do that, I'll tend to Sybil. I'll let you know when you and your daughter can come back in."

Your daughter. The phrase, along with the tiny life he held, filled him with a special love he didn't know existed. All that had seemed wrong in his life before this moment became a distant memory. Holding his daughter, he thanked God for this precious blessing.

The next few weeks were a conflict of joyful moments and heartbreaking disappointments. Lyddie thrived, proving to be a delightful baby. Will watched over her like a daddy red fox over its kit. He diapered her and bathed her, and when Sybil refused any more attempts at breastfeeding, Eleanor showed him how to make a formula from canned milk. He loved feeding times the best. Watching his daughter's mouth as she sucked the bottle and hearing her little gasps of air filled him with awe.

But his concern heightened as he waited for Sybil to mother her daughter. With each passing day, he grew more fearful it might never happen. Thank goodness for Eleanor, who came every day. Each time, she managed to entice Sybil to sit in a chair, and while brushing her hair, she talked to her about sweet Lyddie Anne.

Today, Will stood outside the open bedroom door, holding the sleeping baby in his arms.

"You should see Lyddie today," Eleanor said as she stood brushing Sybil's long, blond hair. "She's a lovely baby. Her cheeks are full and rosy." When no reply came, she continued, "Will just bathed her and wrapped her in a soft pink blanket. Why don't I have him bring her in? You can hold her for a while."

"No, I'm too tired. Maybe I'll hold her tomorrow," Sybil said as she stood from the chair and moved to the bed.

Eleanor shook her head at Will when she left the bedroom. "Maybe tomorrow," she whispered.

"Remember, Dr. Jennings said some mothers have a problem with the baby blues. Don't get discouraged."

There had been too many promises of "tomorrow." With slumped shoulders, Will headed down the stairs. How could a mother not want her child?

Lyddie was two weeks old before Sybil left the bedroom for the first time. Encouraged to see his wife downstairs, Will poured her a cup of coffee and set it on the table.

"Here's a hot cup for you, sweetheart. Lyddie should wake up soon, and she'll be hungry. Would you like to feed her?" His gaze moved to the basket on the table where the baby lay sleeping.

"Not now. We need to talk." She responded without a glance at the child. "I've been thinking. We want the best for our daughter, right?" She turned big doe eyes to her husband.

"Of course we do," he replied, narrowing his eyes. He'd heard this tone of voice before. Always when she wanted something.

"Well, when I think of the best, I know it can't be here. Not in this old farmhouse, miles from a decent town. Our daughter needs to be brought up around refined people in a place where she can learn cultural things." She paused, then continued, her voice full of urgency. "I've had all this time since the baby was born to think about it. And I think the best thing is for me and Lyddie to move back home."

She continued before he could completely process the announcement, much less respond. "Morgantown is a perfect place to raise a child. Why, there's the university, the museum...oh, and did I tell you about the library? One of the best in the state. My mother and father would be happy to have us, and of course you're welcome to come and visit anytime."

Will stared at the table where he sat, not moving a muscle.

"Will? Will! You could at least say something, for goodness' sake. Did you even heard a word I said?"

Raising his head, he pinned her with hard, cold eyes. "Hear me on this, Sybil Parson. Our child will not live in your parent's house. This is her home. We'll have no more talk about it."

He stood and walked to the stove to retrieve a bottle from the hot water bath. "When your daughter wakes up, feed her. I'll be in the apple house." He headed to the back door.

"Don't walk away from me, Will Parson!" Sybil shouted.

The frightened baby woke and let out a piercing cry.

He spun around. "Watch me, Sybil! The baby's awake now. See to her." He left through the kitchen door, ignoring the angry words spewed at his back.

When Will returned at noon, Sybil met him at the back door and shoved the fretful baby into his arms before he'd even washed.

"I can't—I won't do this," she cried, then retreated to the bedroom.

Light from the new-day sun filtered through the lace curtains when Will stood over his sleeping wife. "Get up, Sybil," he said as he laid the sleeping child on the bed next to her mother and backed away. "I'm going to the hives since we have a warm day. I need to harvest the last of this year's honey. Make sure you feed Lyddie when she wakes up."

Fear for the three-week-old's safety threatened to change his mind. Every attempt to get Sybil to care for the baby hadn't worked. His gut told him it was time to take this chance. He started for the door, then paused to make sure Sybil was indeed awake.

She lifted the baby with one arm while grabbing a cigarette with her free hand. "I'll take care of her now, Will. But not for long. I plan to call my parents and ask them to visit. When they know how their daughter and granddaughter are living, they'll make you see why my idea is good."

Will left the room without answering. He wouldn't let his wife see the fear on his face. He hadn't yet told her about the bank run and losing what little money they had, but he'd have to soon. The shortage of cash wouldn't go unnoticed for long.

Lord, don't let her leave. And keep Lyddie safe in her mother's care today. I don't see any other way than forcing her to care for our daughter. And please help me with this money problem.

His conversations with God since the birth of his daughter surprised him. He felt comforted each time he took his fears to God.

Chapter 15

"That's it, Danny. Your hold on the reins is perfect. Reckon this is your best ride ever."

"I ride good, huh, Sam? Sunshine's best horse ever."

"You're the best, Danny-boy," the trainer replied.

Eleanor shaded her eyes from the morning sun, crisp December air filling her lungs as she watched her son on his last ride. She scanned the sky, hopeful the weather would remain calm. Later today, their new owner would arrive to load the horses, and Sam would leave soon after.

She hadn't told Danny they must leave their home next week. How could she explain the economic crisis to her son when she still struggled to understand what had happened over the past weeks? One day they were the owners of a beautiful estate with a secure income; the next, they were homeless and penniless. Her life had become a tilt-a-whirl, keeping her off balance.

Since she put the advertisement in the newspaper, hordes of strangers walked through their home and about the estate, buying items at far less than the price she paid when she purchased them. When the first buyers showed up each morning, Carl left immediately and stayed gone until nightfall, sometimes later. Eleanor had to deal with the logistics of the sales. She knew little about the farm equipment and blessed Sam for helping when someone was interested in something. At least he could try to get them close to a fair price.

It was only a matter of time before Danny would want to know what was happening. Just yesterday, he became upset when he saw a woman leave their kitchen with the Toastmaster toaster, which he used every morning for his toast.

When a truck came to load the Philco cabinet radio, Danny had cried. "But, Mama, what about the Lone Ranger?" He'd tried to get it off the bed of the truck, and when he wasn't successful, he'd disappeared for an entire afternoon. Eleanor herself wanted to cry when her Frigidaire ice box left with a young couple who gushed over their great bargain.

Was it just two weeks ago that Sheriff Eakins came to their door, grim-faced and serious? It felt like a lifetime now as her mind replayed the visit.

"Morning, Eleanor. I'm wondering if we could have a talk."

"Good morning." Her eyes darted to the driveway, knowing Carl would be home soon.

"We can meet on the porch, if you like."

"Goodness no, Benson," she said, taking a deep breath. "It's much too cold. Come on in. I'll get us a cup of coffee."

"No, I can't stay long," he said as they made their way to the parlor. "I need to show you a document." He sat in a chair across from the sofa where she perched on the edge, her back straight, her hands folded.

Instinct warned her that whatever the document said wasn't good. Since the bank closed, she'd waited for the other shoe to drop. Her days now were so unlike the days in her past. Carl was home most of the time now, but he differed from the man she knew. He spent long hours sitting in the parlor, staring out the front window as if expecting someone to come down the drive.

At least he'd not been bullying her or Danny. Most days, he didn't seem to know they were around. She'd tried a few times to draw him out, asking him what his plans were since the bank closed. Each time, he grabbed his hat and left without a word. When he returned late in the night, he'd pass out on the sofa.

"Best let me see what you've brought, please," she said, reaching for the document.

Her chest tightened as she read the words stating that their home and land would be in foreclosure by mid-December—just three weeks away.

"How can this be?" She looked at Benson, her forehead wrinkled with confusion. "This place has been in Carl's family for generations. He owns it outright."

"I'm sorry to be the one to bring this news to you, but I've tried to contact Carl several times. So far, he's ignored my request to see him."

She knew then why Carl refused to let her answer any phone calls when he was home. He'd jump from his chair and race to the phone, often only to hang up without a word.

"But I still don't understand. What is West Virginia Savings and Loan? Why do they say we have a mortgage?"

"Because you do, Eleanor. Carl borrowed on this place last year. At first, he made the payments, but for the last eight months there's been no attempt to pay the mortgage. My understanding is, the savings and loan attempted to contact Carl through letters and phone calls. The president even tried to visit with him at his office before the bank closed. Carl refused to see him."

Slowly, a timeline fell into place like pieces of a puzzle as she recalled multiple phone calls from Johnny to his father, the content of which Carl chose not to share. Then came Carl's endless bragging about his son's great business opportunity. All of this happened slightly over a year ago.

Surely Carl didn't mortgage our home to give Johnny money for one of his trumped-up schemes. Her stomach twisted when she realized this had to be the reason for the foreclosure. *Oh, Carl. What have you done?*

She inhaled and lifted her gaze back to the sheriff. "Thank you for bringing this to me. I can't say for sure why Carl allowed this to happen, but I'll try to make him realize he can't run from it." The words sounded brave, but she trembled at the thought of confronting her husband.

Benson stood to leave. "I'll do whatever I can to help, Eleanor. You know that, right?"

A sudden and unexpected rush of pride filled her and she spoke in a formal tone. "Thank you, Sheriff Eakins. I'll let Carl know you dropped by."

Benson stepped through the door and tipped his hat to Eleanor. "Please see Carl knows about that document. Goodbye, Mrs. Rhode."

Guilt shot through Eleanor. How could she have been so rude to this man? A man who had always treated her far better than her husband did.

Maybe it was that she saw her life crumbling before her. Maybe she enjoyed the position and possessions more than she thought. Conflict raged within her.

Then, like a butterfly in quiet motion, she heard God's soft-spoken whisper. "Daughter, all is well. Accept what is to come. I am your refuge, your help during trouble."

Ashamed, she rushed to the door. "Benson, please wait. There is something...." She held her breath, wondering if he would even turn around after she had acted so poorly. Relief coursed through her when he turned around.

"Of course, anything."

"Well, I was wondering, is it all right to..."

"Just ask. I'll do my best to help." He retraced his steps up the walkway.

"Am I permitted to sell our possessions? I mean, wherever we go, it's not likely we'll need these things. If I could sell some of the household items and even the farm implements, it would help."

"I'm no lawyer, but Carl made the loan with the house and land as collateral, not the possessions. I think you can sell whatever you want, though it isn't likely you'll get much for anything." He paused, then continued. "Might be a good idea to come into town and place an ad in the *Berkley Gazette*. It comes out the day after tomorrow, so you'll have several days to make sales."

"Thank you, Benson. You've been a good friend."

"I wish it were different for you and Danny. Wherever you go, I hope you'll keep in touch. These hard times can't last forever." He tipped his hat a last time and left in his patrol car.

She watched until he turned onto the road. Suddenly, her knees buckled. She needed to sit down as dizziness and nausea threatened to overcome her. How would she tell Carl, and how would he react?

Eleanor shook her head to break her memory of that day. Danny would be in soon, and over lunch she would tell him about their move. But where were they moving? This question had haunted her for days. Any discussion with Carl ended with a sharp word or his storming out of the house.

Unable to communicate with her husband, she'd written to her mother. Maybe they could stay with her family until they found a place. It would be close quarters and Carl would hate it, but she couldn't think of another place to go.

She returned to the kitchen and glanced at the clock. She had time to walk to the mailbox before lunch. The cool morning air might help calm her nerves. Maybe a letter from her folks had arrived.

She said a quick prayer before pulling open the mailbox. There lay a thin envelope in her mother's handwriting.

"Thank you, God," Eleanor whispered as she grabbed the envelope and tore into it. Tears blotted out the words before she finished the letter.

Dear Eleanor,

Your pa and I have tried to find some way to help you. But we can't, sweet child. When the stock market crashed, along with so many banks, it hit the coal industry hard. The mine began laying off workers, and because of his age, your pa was one of the first to go. We must move out of company housing soon.

He searched everywhere for a place to live, but after we settled our debt at the company store, there was almost no cash left.

Then he remembered an old, abandoned houseboat down on the river where he fishes. He's staying there now, so no one else will take it. The rest of us are joining him there tomorrow.

We're blessed to find it when so many miners are looking for a place to live. It's only one room for the seven of us and it's in poor shape, but it will be a roof over our head until these bad times pass.

It breaks my heart to say no to your need,

Eleanor. But we can't see any other way. Maybe your pa will find some work soon so we can move where there's space for you and your family. Until then, write to me at the post office at Pineville.

You'll be in our prayers, dear daughter.

God Bless,

Mama

Eleanor took a step back and her legs turned to jelly. She sat down hard on a patch of grass beside the mailbox. Her hands trembled as she wiped her tears and read the letter again. She vacillated between panic about her own situation and concern for her parents.

They must come here! Before the thought took root, she remembered there wouldn't be a *here* to come to in a few more days. She'd been so hopeful they could go to her parents. Now where would they go?

If only Carl would take charge. Instead, he refused to see reality, preferring to spend his time talking about when Johnny would return, having made his fortune. The mental and emotional fatigue that had shadowed her for days threatened to overtake her.

But as she sat on the cold, hard ground, a strength filled her, a strength she could only believe came from God, as a plan formed in her thoughts. They would use some of the money from the sale of their possessions to live in a hotel until they could find a place to rent. It would give them time to search for a home, and perhaps the move to a hotel would be easier on Carl's pride.

The hammer-hard beats of her heart softened as she remembered something Pastor Grandy said the last time she and Danny visited an evening service. "There's no pit so deep that God is not deeper still."

Chapter 16

*T*illy moved west about eight hundred yards from the spruce near the beehives to another large spruce, thankful for these large, majestic evergreens. She felt more vulnerable in the winter months when so many of the trees lost their foliage. Now, she stood under the low branches of another spruce—a safe place to watch the arena. She came here often to watch Danny and Sam ride. When the wind blew toward the forest, she enjoyed hearing the conversation between them.

Today, the wind was in her favor and she could clearly hear their conversation. Yet, something seemed different from the other times. Sam's words were stiff, and he stopped often to clear his throat. It confused her, as did so much of what she'd observed over the past weeks at both places she secretly watched. Being in the forest had always been as natural as taking her next breath. Now things felt off balance, making her nervous.

"What's happenin'? I feel change is comin'," she whispered. A spark of anxiety caught fire and caused a slow burn within her. *Why are both these families selling their things? Why isn't Will out tending to his orchard and beehives?*

Her heart was no less heavy when she recalled a phrase Big Mama often shared. "In life, strong winds will come. Best to think on the cool breeze that always follows."

With a sigh, she started for the river to meet Josiah. This time of year, when the forest slept for winter, little remained to forage. Thankfully, she had a large stock of poultices and teas, made during the months the woods offered a variety of plants.

She'd asked Josiah to bring bags of flour, cornmeal, baking soda, and coffee, as her bins were getting low. More than this, she hoped he could explain what was happening around her.

The small boat moved to the water's edge as she arrived at the river. She grabbed the rope he threw her direction and tied it to a low branch. Josiah moved slower than Solomon as he picked a wooden box from the bottom of the boat. She folded and unfolded her hands, eager to ask her questions. Yet she knew every movement of his body brought joint pain. It wouldn't be right to ask him to hurry.

Finally, he stood before her with the box. "Mornin', Miz Tilly. I got your stuff here, but not as much as you asked for. Grocery store's mighty low on stock."

"Why's that, Josiah?" In her haste, she by-passed

a greeting and spewed out her question. "Seems like lots of things is different." Words tumbled from her, more words than she usually exchanged as she explained what she saw around her. "What's happening, Josiah?"

"Don't know as I can rightly say. It's confusin'. Some talk about a stock market crashin' and banks closin'. Know for sure the bank in Berkley closed up. Heard lots of people lost they money." He smiled a toothless grin. "Reckon 'hits the first time I ever thanked the Lord for not havin' mo' money!"

His grin melted as he continued. "I fear it might get bad. Lots of folk gettin' laid off at the mine. They's word it might close. Worst is talk o' people movin' off. Sure do hope that don't happen, Miz Tilly. We needs our customers."

Tilly watched Josiah maneuver the boat into the river's current, heading back the way he'd come. Her head was full of the things Josiah had shared. Dread, heavier than her companion of loneliness, gnawed at her. She had no plan for what to do if she could no longer live in her forest.

She walked through the woods without purpose, though she'd intended to harvest mushrooms before returning to the cabin. They were easy to find in the winter months and provided flavor to her soups and stews. Today, her mind couldn't concentrate on the mushrooms. She could only think of what Josiah had told her.

"Be still and know..."

She stopped and crouched low. *Who said that?*

"Be still and know..."

This time she realized it was a thought—but where had it come from and why did she think it?

At bedtime, she still fretted, unable to settle into her nighttime routine as thoughts of all she'd seen, and all Josiah told her, rumbled around in her head. *If ever'body moves away, what'll become of me?* The thought threatened to squeeze the air from her lungs.

Though she wouldn't be sad to see the Rhode family leave. Her mind wondered back to the last day she had lived with Big Mama in the big house. The boy persuaded her to come to the garden shed. "There's a mama kitten there with five new kittens. You can have the pick of the litter," he'd said with a kindness that dissipated when he closed the shed door.

Shame and anger once again flooded her. *I shouldn't'a gone—that's what Big Mama said.* But she had, and her life changed course that day.

Now she feared it would change again.

Rising from where she sat, she whispered, "I reckon I might as well go to bed, Solomon. I ain't likely to figure out anything tonight."

Sometime past midnight, Tilly woke from a restless sleep. Her first thought was *Psalm 46.* She took a moment to shake off her sleepiness when the same phrase flitted through her mind, like a butterfly moving from one bit of nectar to the next.

She scrambled out of bed and scurried outside to the cellar, glad there was a full moon to light the path. Inside, she felt her way to the hiding place behind the box of potatoes. Pushing the box aside, she searched with her hand until she found Big Mama's Bible. She had hidden it here when Big Mama died, no longer interested in the God she figured had abandoned her.

Back in the cabin, she lit her lantern and pulled the Bible onto her lap. It took some searching to find the book of Psalms. But when she did, there in Psalm 46:10, she read, *Be still and know that I am God.*

Confused, she tried to remember where she'd heard this verse before. Was it from Big Mama, or had she heard it in church? Try as she might, she couldn't remember.

She moved on to verse eleven. *The Lord of hosts is with us; the God of Jacob is our refuge.*

She reached for a tattered dictionary Big Mama had given her with the words, "No reason to grow up ignor'nt just 'cause you stuck in these woods." She pushed the pages back and forth until she found what she was searching for. Refuge—a safe place, sheltered from pursuit, danger, or trouble.

Her eyes moved back to the Bible, which lay open on her lap. She lifted it closer to her face and leaned into the glow of the lantern. Backtracking from verse ten, she landed on verse one. *God is our refuge and strength, a very present help in trouble.*

Tilly continued to read one Psalm after another, each one feeding her hungry soul. As the night gave way to the soft rays of morning, the darkness in her heart melted with the realization she'd never once been alone in her forest. Regardless of what the winds of change might bring, she knew now she'd face it with the Lord.

Chapter 17

*T*he sound of a vehicle coming up the drive pulled Sybil to the window. Relieved to see Eleanor and Danny coming up the walk, she hurried to meet them at the door.

"Eleanor, I'm so glad you're here. The baby's been asleep for three hours." Sybil wrung her hands together. "Do you think she's all right? I'm so afraid I might do something wrong. I just don't think I can do this."

"Calm down, Sybil. I'll run up there and check." Eleanor put the box she was carrying in the chair by the door. "Danny, you keep Miss Sybil company. I'll be right back."

Danny watched his mother rush up the stairs, then turned to Sybil. "We brung you peaches. I sad. Horses gone. Sam too."

Sybil watched as Eleanor climbed the stairs,

hoping she would come back down soon. She never knew what to say or how to act around Danny.

His usually cheerful face did indeed seem sad. Her heart softened, and she put her hand on Danny's shoulder. "Why don't you help me put these jars of peaches in the kitchen? I need them on a high shelf. I'll bet you can reach it better than me."

Danny brightened. "I help good."

Eleanor found them in the pantry as Sybil instructed Danny where to put the jars of peaches.

"I help, Mama."

"I see that. Thank you, son." Eleanor smiled at Danny before she turned to Sybil. "Lyddie is fine. She's older now and eating more. A full tummy helps her sleep longer."

"I get so scared, Eleanor. I never know if I'm doing the right things. And every time I hold her, she cries. You and Will are the only two she wants."

"We've talked about this before. Babies sense tension. You need to relax, and she'll soon take to you like she has to Will."

"What am I going to do when you leave? I can't manage without you."

"We've talked about this too," Eleanor sighed. "You must believe that you can be a mother to Lyddie and a wife to Will. There's lots of love here for you to receive, but you must learn to give it as well."

"I know. But I've been so upset since I talked with my mother. I can hardly think what to do sometimes."

The phone call to her parents had not gone well. She'd been sure they would rush to Applewood Orchard at her bidding. They always had before. Never had she heard a "no" from the mouth of either parent.

The details of why they couldn't come got muddled up in her thoughts of herself. In a fit of temper, she'd slammed the receiver back on the hook with a loud clank.

When she replayed her mother's story after the call ended, she accepted they wouldn't come. Couldn't come. When the college began laying off professors to reduce their payroll in these hard economic times, her father lost his job. Her parents were forced to move out of the college housing and all their savings went away when their bank closed. They were living with her mother's aunt in a small country home twenty miles from the college town.

After she calmed down, Sybil realized how sad and beaten her mother had sounded. She felt sorry for them, but it didn't help her circumstances. She'd muddled through the last several weeks, but only with the help of Eleanor. And now her trusted friend would be leaving.

Will walked through the kitchen door and pulled Sybil from her thoughts.

"Mr. Will, my horses go away. Sam, too," shouted Danny.

"I know, buddy. I'm sure sorry about that."

"It's okay. Mama say someday we get more horses." Danny shrugged his shoulder. "Mr. Will, when someday come?"

"Danny, if I knew that, I'd be a rich man for sure."

"You funny, Mr. Will. Just like Sam."

Eager to move the conversation back to herself, Sybil said, "Eleanor brought us some jars of peaches. They're leaving tomorrow, Will." She worked hard to not put her lip out in a pout.

"I know, Sybil. That's why I came in from the orchard. I wanted to say goodbye."

A sudden sharp cry from upstairs startled her. "The baby's awake," she announced.

Neither Will nor Eleanor moved. She waited a minute more, then huffed, "Oh, all right! I'll go get her."

She moved up the stairs, whispering, "Relax. Don't be tense and she won't cry." At the top of the stairs, she realized the cries had stopped. "Maybe she's gone back to sleep."

She tiptoed into the room and crept to the crib. Lyddie lay on her back with one foot in her hands. She tried with all her might to get the toes of her right foot into her mouth. Sybil let out a soft giggle at the cuteness of it.

Lyddie moved her attention from her toes and locked her eyes with those of her mother's. Her child gave her a wide grin.

"Silly, you mustn't eat your toes. You'll need them one day for the dances I plan to teach you," she whispered, delighted by the attention her daughter gave her. *Such a pretty child. My hair and chin, but Will's soft blue eyes.* She wanted to stand there longer, but she needed to go back downstairs before Eleanor left.

"I have to take you downstairs now, Lyddie Anne. Do you think, just this once, you could not cry? Let Daddy see you happy in my arms, please." She lifted Lyddie into her arms while holding her breath and paused for a second as she waited for the wails to come. But they didn't. Lyddie reached for a lock of Sybil's long hair and kept her eyes on her mother.

Sybil's heart melted like butter in a hot pan. Love for her daughter filled her from head to toe. At that moment, she'd have fought a mountain lion to keep her daughter safe and happy.

She walked into the kitchen with all the pride of a runner crossing the finish line first. With tears in her eyes, she stood before Will. "She didn't cry when I picked her up. She smi... she smiled at me." Her voice cracked as a tear made a slow trip down her cheek.

"Oh, Eleanor, you're right. I need to be calm. Isn't she cute? Look at her pretty little lips. And see how her hair already wants to curl. And guess what? Lyddie held onto my hair." She turned back to Will then. "Do you think she knows I'm her mother? It'd be wonderful if she did."

"Of course, she knows you're her mother. She's a smart girl, and a pretty one too."

Eleanor reached and hugged both mother and baby. "I'm proud of you. Now I can leave without worrying about you or Lyddie."

Danny clapped both hands and said, "She good baby. Maybe give her peaches!"

"I've a favor to ask before we leave," Eleanor said, looking from Sybil to Will. "If Johnny comes home, please tell him he can find us at the Mountainview Motel in Davis. We're staying there until we can find a house to rent. If he doesn't come soon, tell him I'll leave our new address at the desk of the motel. We can't stay there long; our money will run out."

She cast her eyes to the floor, then back to Will. "I know Carl hasn't always treated you the best. But he's struggling in these times. It's harder for him than it is for Danny and me."

"Of course we'll make sure Johnny knows where to find you," Will said, and Sybil nodded her agreement.

"Danny, go tell Daisy goodbye. She's over near our car." Eleanor moved her gaze back to Sybil. "I'm so pleased with what happened today, Sybil. I don't think you'll struggle with Lyddie so much now. But know this. God's hand was over what happened in the baby's room today. He wants you and Will to be a happy family, a family that glorifies Him. For sure, hard times will come in your marriage, but He promises to be with you in the good and in the bad. Let Him be the fourth member of this family."

Sybil nodded. "I'll try. I promise." She held the baby even closer, her eyes moist.

"And you, Will. You need to turn back to God. He never left you. You left him."

They stood on the front porch, watching Eleanor's car bounce down the drive. It saddened Sybil to know Eleanor no longer had a home—just like her parents and so many others.

"I'll miss her so much. But I promise to try to be a good mother and a good wife." For the first time in months, Sybil stepped close to her husband, laying a hand on his arm. "And I want you to know I'm happy to have this drafty old farmhouse. Now, let's go in. Lyddie doesn't need to be out here in the cold."

Chapter 18

*W*ill bent over the ledger, his back tight, his head throbbing. He'd worked on the farm accounts since dinner and still didn't know how to settle the debts. What he owed exceeded the cash he had. How would he pay for these debts and have the funds to pay Juan for his help with the winter pruning?

He sighed, then listened to Sybil's chatter from the parlor. She'd had Lyddie on a pallet near the fire, talking and playing with her, for the past hour. He smiled, thankful she'd become less frightened about caring for the baby. In fact, she devoted her waking hours to Lyddie's needs and little else.

He glanced at the state of the kitchen. Dirty dishes sat piled high in the sink, and the floor needed mopping. Laundered clothes lay drying on every piece of furniture. More than likely, he'd be the one to fold and put them away. Still, he couldn't get aggravated with Sybil when things were so much better now.

A knock brought him back from his thoughts.

Sybil turned her head briefly but remained on the floor next to the baby. "Who would visit this time of night?"

Will opened the door, surprised to see his old friend Tom standing there in a well-worn coat and a cap he'd probably had when they were in high school together.

"Evening, Tom. Come in out of the cold."

"Will." Tom nodded as he swept the cap from his head. "Sorry to come by so late." He glanced at Sybil and the baby, then ducked his head and asked in a soft voice. "Can we visit a bit—alone?"

"Sure. Come into the kitchen." He grabbed clothes from the chairs around the table and threw them into the basket sitting on the counter. "Sorry, today's laundry day. Couldn't get them dry with the rain and snow we've had all day. Can I get you a cup of coffee?"

"No, but thanks. I won't take up much of your time. I came..." Tom's eyes landed on the bills spread out on the table.

Will hastily pulled the papers into a messy pile. "I've been working on our budget. I try to keep ahead of it." His heart skipped a beat as he hoped his friend hadn't seen the red SECOND NOTICE stamped on several of the bills.

He chastised himself. Tom was his oldest friend, and they normally kept nothing from each other. Besides, both families struggled financially, just like others in the county.

"What brings you out on a night like this?"

"Did you hear the mine laid off miners?"

"Yeah, but I didn't think it would be you. You've

been working there for—what, sixteen, seventeen years now?"

"Eighteen. Didn't seem to matter. Management kept the miners at a lower salary." Tom's shoulders sagged as he sat with his legs spread wide, elbows on his thighs and his cap held between his knees. "Word is the mine'll shut down by spring."

His friend looked broken, but Tom had lots of pride. Sympathy wouldn't do at this moment. Will held his tongue and waited to hear more.

After a moment, Tom's gaze moved back to him. "I'm here to ask for work, Will. I'll do anything. I'm a hard worker, you know that."

"You know I'd do anything to help, but I don't have any extra work. Juan will be here Monday morning to start tree trimming. Truthfully, I don't know how I'll pay him. I'm hoping he'll wait for his pay until the harvest in the fall."

"That's why I came tonight. I saw Juan today. He, his family, and all their possessions were packed in his old truck. They're headed to California. He had a flyer advertising winter crops ready for harvest and needing pickers."

Tom stopped for a moment, then continued. "He asked me to tell you he's sorry to leave, but he needs cash now. I can help with the pruning. You can pay me in the fall. Emma still has her job at the café, and we can get by on that. I just need to be busy about something."

Will took a moment to digest all he'd heard. It had been a long shot to think of asking Juan to wait for his pay, but Will figured he owed his friend and worker of five years the opportunity to work. He'd hoped their strong relationship would see them through this time together. The thought of not having Juan to help with all the chores involved in getting a crop of apples harvested made him weak-kneed.

He looked at Tom, who'd always been there for him, good times and bad. "I'd be glad to have help next week. It's hard work, I'll warn you."

"Hard work I'm used to. It's no work that gets me down." Tom grinned his big sloppy grin and pulled his full weight up from the table. "I'll say good night. See you early Monday morning." He tipped his cap at Sybil as he let himself out the front door.

Will remained at the table, looking at the stack of bills but still thinking about his friend. *Lord, let me be able to pay this man come fall. Thank you for providing him.*

"Will, you've been in that kitchen forever. Come see how Lyddie's eyes follow her bear when I move it across her face. She's so smart!"

Will sighed. He walked from the kitchen to the parlor and watched Sybil playing with the baby. Touching as it was, he needed to apprise her of Tom's visit.

"Tom Grimes will start working here starting next week. It's time to prune the trees. I'll need you to get lunch for us every day while he's here." Will paused, then continued, "Maybe you could practice some this week on your stew. The last you made needed more seasoning and more cooking time."

Sybil opened her mouth to respond when another knock came at the door. "Gracious, how many visitors will we have tonight?" This time, curiosity got the best of her, and she rose to go with Will to the door.

Both blinked at the dapper-looking young man in a dark blue pin-striped suit, shiny wingtip shoes, and a bowler hat.

"I'm Johnny Rhode. I've a few questions I need answered." He strolled past Will and Sybil and made his way to the warmth of their fire without an invitation. He didn't spare a glimpse for the baby on the floor beside him.

Will recovered first. "Welcome, Mr. Rhode. I'm..."

"No time for pleasantries. I've been to my parents' home. It's empty and there's a foreclosure sign on the fence. What in God's name happened?" His black eyes drilled into Will's.

Uncomfortable at having to tell the young man of his parents' misfortune, Will stammered, "Uh, I think, um..."

"Spit it out, man. I don't make it a habit to spend my time with country farmers. Just tell me where they are!"

Will's fists closed, opened, and closed again. "Now, look here, Mr. Rhode, there's no need for..."

"Here, this is the address where your parent should be." Sybil extended a slip of paper to Johnny. "They left it with us in case you came back. Eleanor said if they left there, she'd leave a new address at the hotel desk."

Johnny stared at Sybil as though seeing her for the first time. "Oh. Well, I still want to know why they left. None of it makes sense."

Will spoke up then, his lips tight, his voice only slightly controlled. "I'd suggest you wait and speak to your parents about why they left. It's best you hear the reason from them. Is there anything else we can do for you, Mr. Rhode?" He turned and started for the door, hoping the young man would follow.

"Really, Will. Don't be rude. Maybe Johnny would like something hot to drink before going out in the cold again," Sybil said, as she offered a wide smile to Carl's son.

"No. I'm sure our guest needs to be on his way now." Will twisted the knob and cracked the door open. "It's late." He pinned their guest with his eyes.

"Yes, it appears I'll get no more help here." Johnny turned to give Sybil a smile. "Mother never told me she had such a charming neighbor."

"Oh, you're too kind, sir." Sybil twisted a lock of her hair and glanced at the floor.

She moved to the window to watch his vehicle leave, its red rear lights reflecting off the accumulated snow. "Will Parson, our first decent visitor in weeks and you all but push him out the door."

Will didn't respond. His gut tightened as he watched Sybil at the window. The old fear reared its ugly head once again.

Chapter 19

*T*he gray, heavy clouds did little to help Will's spirits. Winter hung on longer than usual this year, and the farmhouse grew tighter each day the weather forced him indoors, like a shirt long outgrown.

To worsen matters, Sybil became whiny again. She spent hours with old magazines, staring at everything from nightgowns to kitchen rugs. At six months, Lyddie needed more care, which didn't seem to suit Sybil. She often pushed the child off on Will with the excuse of a headache. Will knew little about babies, but his daughter seemed exceptionally good, always following her parents' movements with large, blue eyes and offering big smiles.

The days spent shut inside from the cold, damp weather with an unhappy wife wore on Will's nerves. Today, he determined to go to his beehives. He needed to flex his muscles more than he needed to check on the hives. With the temperatures still chilly, he didn't think the bees would swarm, but it offered a plausible reason to be out of the house.

"Sybil, wake up. I'm going to the beehives. I need to check for signs of swarming. Lyddie's had her breakfast and is playing on the rug in the kitchen where it's warm." He waited a moment, not getting a response. "Sybil, did you hear me? Time to get up."

Sybil turned to face him, then threw her arm across her head. "Oh, Will, my head hurts so badly," she moaned. "I can't take care of her now. Not with this throbbing between my eyes." She rolled back over, and Will knew there'd be no getting her out of bed.

"I'll take her with me, then," he said with a sigh. He went to the wardrobe and pulled a quilt from the top shelf. "I can wrap her up and put her in my wagon."

"Uh-huh," Sybil mumbled from under the covers.

Once he'd put warm clothes on the baby, including a sweater and cap Eleanor crocheted for her, he snuggled her into the red wagon. By the time he'd pulled the wagon with one hand and hauled his equipment with the other, a fine sheen of sweat covered his face even though the temperature spoke more of early March than mid-April.

As he suspected, there were no signs of a swarm. Still, the hives could use a good cleaning. A glance at the wagon confirmed Lyddie napped. He cleaned dead leaves off the top and around the edges of the bee boxes and removed sticks which had fallen from the nearby oaks. Busy work, really, but he enjoyed the fresh air.

He glanced at the forest frequently, wondering if someone might be watching or if he was just being foolish. He never shook the feeling of someone nearby when at the beehives. And someone or something had taken the jar of honey he'd left so many months ago.

When he could find no more small chores to do, he considered taking Lyddie home through the apple orchard. He wanted to show her his trees and tell her the story of how her family came to live at Applewood Orchard.

A glance at the clouds told him they didn't have time. The air had become cooler and the clouds darker. He gathered his rake and other items and walked the shortest distance to the house. Snow started before they reached the tool shed. He leaned over and brushed off Lyddie's face, smiling when she blinked as snowflakes landed on her eyelashes. He covered her with the quilt and hurried home.

Sybil appeared when he was putting Lyddie down for a nap. "Will, it's snowing again. How could it? It's the middle of April!" She poured some coffee, picked up one of her well-worn magazines, and retreated to the living room.

He shook his head, trying to not get angry. Then he put on his cap and called over his shoulder, "I'm going to the apple house. Watch the baby."

For the rest of the morning, he puttered about finding odd jobs as he watched the snow accumulate from the wide-open doors.

"Will!" The agonized scream from the house sent him running.

"Oh, no. Lord, no!" Sybil stood near the stove, her eyes glued to Lyddie, full of fear.

He took in the scene in an instant. Lyddie played on a quilt on the floor with her back to Sybil. The only thing out of place seemed to be a big frying pan lying on the floor. "What's wrong? Stop screaming and tell me what's wrong!"

"Oh, Will, Lyddie Anne is deaf! Our baby can't hear a thing."

He stood as still as a statue, trying to assess what he'd just heard.

"Will, have you gone deaf, too? I'm telling you, Lyddie can't hear!"

When he found his voice, Will attempted to calm his frantic wife. "That's impossible. You scared me half to death. I thought something horrible had happened. Whatever made you scream like that?"

"You just watch, you'll see." She picked up the skillet from the floor and let it drop behind the baby from waist high. Lyddie sat still, chewing on her teething toy. She never flinched or turned toward the loud noise.

Fear crept up Will's spine even as he told himself, *not possible—not possible.* He walked over, stood beside the baby, and snapped his fingers near her left ear. No response. Then he knelt behind her and clapped his hands hard in quick succession. Still no response.

"Oh, Will, she's deaf. That's why she follows us with her eyes and hardly ever cries. How will I teach her to dance if she can't hear the music?" Sybil rushed to the sofa, howling.

Unable to take his eyes from his daughter, his shoulders slanted down, hands limp at his side. "Can this be? No, it can't be right!"

Scenes of his daughter played in his mind, like pages turned in a book. Her sweet disposition, never cranky, never crying when sounds should have startled her. The reality took root and began a slow growth in his mind.

He willed himself to go comfort Sybil where she had curled herself into a ball on the sofa. Gathering her in his arms, he shushed her over and over. "We don't know for sure, Sybil." But in his heart of hearts, he knew. Lyddie Anne was deaf.

"We have to take her to a doctor. We have to see if it can get fixed!" Sybil pushed back from him and grabbed his arms with both her hands. "I'll bet they can fix this. It's probably just an ear infection. Do you think?"

"Maybe. I'll call Dr. Jennings."

"No, it can't be a country doctor. Take her to a specialist, Will. The best. That's the least we can do for our daughter."

Will's heart sank. Where would he get the funds to do that? But when he examined his wife's face, he couldn't tell her no. "All right, Sybil. I'll take her to a specialist."

"The best. Do you promise?"

"Yes, I promise. The best."

Chapter 20

*W*ill lay awake long after Sybil cried herself to
sleep. His mind ran a gamut from denial to a
resolve to do anything he could, even sell the orchard,
to help his daughter. He tried to pray but ended up
fussing at God more than praying. How could this be
when he'd just learned to trust again? How could a
loving God let this happen?

He wrestled his demons until a faint light crept
through the bedroom window, daylight enough for
him to see the chest at the foot of the bed. He stood,
careful not to disturb his wife, and knelt before
the antique chest. It made the trip with his great
grandparents from Ohio many years ago. Somewhere
among the keepsakes, there lay a cameo brooch.
Grandfather Parson bought it for Will's grandmother
at the 1883 World's Fair in Chicago while stationed
there as a sailor.

He found the brooch in a soft cotton pouch, tied

with a bit of crocheted lace. He took it and an 1857 Colt revolver, brought by his grandfather when he mustered out of the Navy. He wasn't even sure it would shoot.

Who might buy these items? Money grew tighter for everyone as the Depression dragged on. Finally able to pray, he stayed on his knees long enough to whisper, "God, I need your help with this. Who will buy these things? I need you to get me to those people today!"

Will dressed quietly and left the house without even a cup of coffee. He put the brooch and pistol in the truck's seat, then went to get several bushels of apples and jars of honey from the cellar. He hated to take from his dwindling supply, especially with groceries getting harder to come by. But he would do whatever it took to get help for Lyddie.

A few miles from home, he glanced at the fuel gauge. "How could I have forgotten?" The needle rested just a hair above empty. For a second, he considered turning back. Maybe he could siphon some gasoline from the tractor's tank.

Something kept him going ahead. *Trust?* Maybe; but in his mind, it would take more than trust to get him to Berkley on fumes—it would take a miracle. Still, he continued with only a slight thought of how he'd get home if he didn't sell some of his items.

"Okay, God. It's you, me, and the gas tank. Take me where I need to go." He listened for the tell-tale sound of sputtering from his gas tank as he drove.

Matilda Stotler. Will's head jerked when a name flitted across his mind. *Matilda Stotler, the lawyer's widow?*

He'd only met Matilda Stotler once, at the county fair where she fussed over the entry of her prized rose bush. His mother waggled him into viewing the flower exhibit with her, though he'd rather pick fleas off his dog than venture into the tent filled with blooming flowers and bustling women.

Could this be where he should start? When he'd mentioned the pompous air of Mrs. Stotler that day at the fair, his mother was quick with a reprimand. "Give her some grace, Will. You don't have any idea what it's like to live with Horace Stotler. She's always been kind to me and is fond of your honey."

With a destination in mind, he pressed the gas pedal as fast as his fumes would take him. Her home sat at the end of what the locals called "Powder and Puff Street." He had no problem finding the large Victorian painted lady house splattered in shades of lavender, pink, maroon, green, and ivory.

He paused before the mammoth door, not sure whether to knock or pull the cord that disappeared to the other side of the door. *Maybe I should go to the back entrance?* He took a step back when the door flung open and a large woman in a long, black dress glared at him.

"Well, ring the bell or not! It's your choice. And I'm not giving handouts today. If I had a dime for every beggar that came to my door these days, I'd put an end to this Depression single handedly."

Will stiffened. "I'm not here to beg, ma'am. I've a few things to sell if you're interested."

"Aren't you Sarah Parson's son?" Matilda plucked the spectacles pinned to her bosom and placed them on her nose. She stared hard at Will's face.

"Yes, ma'am. I'm Will."

"Hmm. Never a greater saint than your mother, son. And she set a great store by you. Told me so many times."

Will fumbled with his hat, not sure how to respond.

"Well, go get whatever it is you have in that truck. Let's see if any of it is worth having."

"They're right here, Mrs. Stotler." He pulled the cameo from the small bag in his shirt pocket and reached into his back pocket for the revolver.

"Oh, my!" Matilda gasped. "Now those are as different as night and day. I'm sorry. I don't have a use for either of those. My Horace gave me enough jewelry when he was alive to last me two lifetimes. And what would I do with a revolver? I'd probably shoot myself with it." She paused, then continued, "From what I hear, no one in this county can afford to buy anything. Good luck to you, Will." With that, she slowly closed the door.

Back at the truck, he grabbed a jar of honey, raced to the front door, and sat it against the doorframe.

Then he sat in the truck, afraid to start the engine. What if he'd only had enough gas to get to this house? Would the engine even turn over? Finally, he put his foot on the clutch and pressed the starter, and let out a loud puff of breath when it started.

Will drove back to the square with the hope he might sell the apples and honey to shoppers. Maybe he'd get enough to buy some gas for the trip home. Without the sale of the items from the chest, he'd have no money for a specialist. The thought of telling Sybil he couldn't keep his promise made him nauseous.

He parked in front of the dentist's office since few people had the money for a visit regardless of how bad the toothache might be. He wanted to be well away from O'Bryan's Mercantile so as not to take business from Sean.

As he waited for customers, Will sat on his tailgate, whittling a toy for Lyddie from a stick he'd found. No one stopped or even glanced his way, as if it embarrassed them to not have the funds to purchase even a single apple.

"Not going to be any sales today," he muttered to himself a few hours later. "Maybe Jode will lend me just enough gas to get home." As he put his whittling in the cab, a grinding of gears came from behind the truck, ending in a screech of brakes. Mrs. Stotler's car rolled to a stop perilously close to his truck.

"I never did like to drive this car of Horace's. Too many things to push!" she said, fanning herself with her hankie as she got out of the car. "Now, Will Parson, I did some thinking after you left. My Horace never did like banks. Said they weren't to be trusted and, being a lawyer, I reckon he'd know who he could trust and who he couldn't. Few years before he passed, he took most of his savings out of the bank and buried them.... Well, I guess you don't need to know that! I didn't lose much when the bank closed. In fact, I may have more money than good sense."

She caught her breath, then continued. "Your mother was the closest thing I had to a friend in this town. I don't know if I deserved her friendship, but it's true. And I did very little to return it before she passed." She dabbed her eyes with the hankie. "I'm here to change that. I'll give you twenty dollars apiece for the brooch and revolver."

She glanced over at the produce in the truck's bed. "And I'll give you another ten for those apples and jars of honey. I help with the soup line at the Presbyterian church. Some stewed apples might be an excellent side dish with the stew."

Will felt as if the latches in his mind had gone rusty. Was she saying she planned to buy everything, and for so large an amount? Words formed in the back of his throat, but they didn't make it to his lips.

Matilda put both palms on her huge hips. "Well, do you want me to load these items in this cantankerous old car myself, or didn't you mother raise you better?"

He had a powerful urge to hug the woman right there on the square.

Once she'd supervised the loading, she turned back to him. "Son, I know whatever trouble brought you to my door this morning is serious. If it has anything to do with your daughter, and I suspect it does, then I want you to know I'll be praying for her every time I wear this brooch, which will be often." She smiled, then got into the driver's seat and said, "Now go on over to Jode's and get yourself some gasoline. You'll need it to get home."

Will watched the car jerk and wheeze out of sight, his mouth hanging open. *How did she know I need gasoline?*

Chapter 21

*M*etal ground against metal and the train lurched forward. Will held Lyddie close, hoping the noise wouldn't wake her. Then he remembered.

The appointment took twenty minutes. Less than half an hour to pronounce a lifetime of silence. Will heard the words of the specialist as though he stood in a tunnel. "Profoundly deaf. Probably from the difficult birth. Keep her home until she is three, then she should go to live at the school for the deaf in Romney."

Will looked down at the sleeping child in his arms, at her sweet cupid mouth and golden curls, a miniature match to her mother. She'd been asleep even before they boarded, exhausted from the early morning train ride and the doctor's examination. He couldn't imagine sending her away to a school. Romney was less than fifty miles from Berkley, but it might as well have been on the moon. No way would he ever let his daughter be raised by someone else.

As the train made its way through narrow valleys and wound around the side of mountains, he stared out the window, unable to enjoy the scenery. He could only think of what Lyddie's life might be like. Would she be able to go to school in Berkley with hearing students? How would she learn? How could he keep her safe? His mind raced, leaving him emotionally exhausted.

Will envied her sleep, something he'd missed this past week. Finding a specialist, planning for a trip to Charleston, and trying to keep Sybil calm left every molecule of his body sapped of energy. Now, he must go home and tell her what the specialist said.

Part of him wished Sybil had gone with him to hear the words herself. But another part was glad she hadn't heard about the cause being a difficult childbirth. Would she blame herself? Or him, claiming "If you hadn't brought me to the god-forsaken place...?" He feared she might take to the idea of sending Lyddie to the school.

Maybe I'll just tell her Lyddie is profoundly deaf and the doctor doesn't know why. As soon as he had the thought, his gut clenched. *No, it would be wrong to lie to Sybil. She's Lyddie's mother and has a right to know.* He would tell her exactly what the doctor had told him and deal with the school when Lyddie was closer to age three.

He laid his head on the back of the train bench and willed sleep to come. It didn't. Instead, the phrase *profoundly deaf* replayed over and over in his mind.

Will left the train and hoofed it to the truck before Lyddie woke up. He'd hope she'd stay asleep until he got home since he had no more milk for her bottle. The hope evaporated when she made it known she woke and cried out with hunger.

Instead of driving out of town, he pulled into the diner. He'd buy her some milk and have a strong cup of coffee before he took the news home to Sybil.

Every head turned when Will walked into the diner with a screaming baby.

"Hello. What are you and Lyddie doing out at this time of day?" Emma said as she walked up to the booth Will snagged by the door. "And her all dressed up in those fine baby clothes. From the sound of it, this child knows it's suppertime."

"Hi, Em... Emma," he stammered, not ready to share the news about Lyddie Anne, but with no other reason for being in town with the baby at dusk. "Maybe you could get me some warm milk for her and sit a minute. I'll tell you why while I feed her."

Emma returned within minutes with the milk and a cup of coffee. "You look like you could use this," she said as she slid into the booth across from him.

"Thank you. I reckon we both need a boost." He filled the baby bottle and offered it to Lyddie, who grabbed it with both hands and sucked hard. Will took a long swallow of the coffee, then turned to Emma with a sigh.

"I've been to see a doctor in Charleston. A hearing specialist. He told me Lyddie Anne is profoundly deaf." Will paused, not knowing what to say next. It felt more real now he'd said it, but he didn't want pity, not from Emma or from anyone.

Emma's expression never changed. She looked at Lyddie, who stared back as she drank from her bottle. She leaned in closer and put the tip of her right thumb on her forehead, her palm and fingers wide open. Then she pointed at Will and said "Father."

To Will's surprise, her fingers flew as she watched Lyddie. When she stopped, she turned to Will.

"I know how devastated you must feel right now," she said. "But please trust me when I say Lyddie can still have a good life—a full life. I just told her this. She's too young to learn sign language now, but before long, she'll chatter so much, you'll want to put mittens on her."

She gave a small laugh before she continued. "My mother was deaf. My father and all us kids learned sign language." Then she became serious. "I know this is tough news. But trust me, Lyddie will do just fine in a hearing world. My mother did. Now, can I bring you our special? It's meatloaf."

When he found his voice, he said softly, "No. I'd best get on home. Sybil is waiting to hear what the doctor said. She's been mighty upset. So upset she has one of her headaches, so she couldn't go with us today. She won't take this news well, I fear."

"No, I don't think she will," Emma said with a sigh. "I'm off on Thursday. Why don't I come out for a visit? It might help her to know some about the deaf community."

"That'd be great. Bring Tom with you. I have the money to pay him for his help with the tree trimming."

"Uh, I think he'll be busy," she said, eyes cast down at the table.

"Did he find a job? Where's he working?"

Emma stood and grabbed the empty coffee cup and milk glass. Then she pulled a cloth from her apron pocket and wiped the table. "Oh, you know how it goes. If there's no steady job, my Tom's going to find odd jobs to do here and there. That man never could be still."

Concern for his friend built up in Will's chest at Emma's reluctance to share more. He'd heard money was still good for whiskey runners and hoped his friend wasn't doing anything illegal. Then he remembered hearing about some men who were mining in shafts that had shut down. Dangerous work, but there was a black market for coal. The biggest danger came from the build up of methane gas, which could explode.

Whatever his friend might be doing, the crowded diner wasn't the place to talk about it. He gathered Lyddie in his arms and stood to leave but turned to share a last thought with Emma. "The doctor said she should go to a school for the deaf in Romney when she's three."

Emma's gentle face turned hard. "Don't take her there, Will. Don't even think about it." She headed to the back of the diner without another word.

Will watched her back, perplexed. Whatever her thoughts about the school, he'd ask later when she was ready to share.

Night had fallen before Will arrived back at home. He sat in the truck, where Lyddie had fallen back to sleep in the seat next to him. A mass of bright stars shown through the windshield. He usually enjoyed the night sky as he searched for planets and different constellations. Tonight, nothing seemed the same. Could he teach his daughter about the stars if she couldn't hear him? The dread which had started when he left the doctor's office now consumed him.

How do I tell Sybil that Lyddie will never hear her mother's voice?

When the baby squirmed, he knew he couldn't put off going inside any longer. He bundled Lyddie in the soft pink blanket Sybil had insisted he bring. "I don't want anyone to think we aren't providing for her. April's a funny month. The weather can go from warm to cool in minutes." Will had bitten back the words, *Then you come along and take care of her.*

He stepped onto the porch when the door opened. Sybil stood there, wringing her hands, evidence of a day's worth of tears on her face. "Tell me now. Can they fix it?"

Will shook his head and reached out with the baby, expecting her to want her daughter. Instead, Sybil turned and walked up the staircase. He heard the door to their bedroom close before he entered the house.

The next week was a mad scramble of caring for the baby as Will juggled the farm work around Lyddie's schedule. He spent long moments at their bedroom door as he tried to coax Sybil to come out. Of all the reactions Will expected from Sybil, this silent mask of indifference wasn't one of them.

Eventually, he persuaded her to leave their room when he announced, "I have to harvest my spring honey. I can't take Lyddie with me. She might get stung, so you must keep her. With sugar in short supply, people will want to buy our honey and we need the cash."

So began a routine. When Will worked outside, Sybil took care of the baby. As soon as he came back into the house, she handed him Lyddie and headed upstairs.

Every evening Emma could spare, she came to Applewood Orchard to teach Will sign language. Soon he learned several words like dog, cat, angry, and hungry. His favorite words were apple and tree. Gradually a hope built in him. Maybe he could talk with his daughter about Applewood Orchard after all.

Chapter 22

"Sybil, wake up," Will said as he pushed on his wife's shoulder. "I'm headed to the garden. I'll be back in soon for breakfast. Please get Lyddie up and fed."

Only a moan came from beneath the covers. "Sybil, I'm serious. Wake up now. The baby's already awake. She needs tending to, and I have to get the produce picked if we're to have any sales today." He shoved a little harder on her shoulder, causing her to jerk back.

"I don't know why you have to be in the garden at the crack of dawn," Sybil whined as she peeked her head from under the bedsheet. "Who's going to drive by your stand this early?"

"You know we need to take every opportunity to sell our vegetables. Someone might drive by and stop. They won't do that if I'm not out there." Will grabbed his boots and sat on the side of the bed. "Get up, now. Lyddie will be hungry at any moment." The bed springs bounced up and down as he put on first one boot then the other.

"Okay, I'm up. You don't have to shake the bed like it's a boat in water." Sybil stood and grabbed her robe. "I'll get Lyddie fed and dressed and have some breakfast ready when you come in. But I can't keep her all day. When you harvested your honey, I spent hours with her. It exhausted me. It scares me to know something might happen since she can't hear. I'm afraid to turn away for a second."

Will softened his voice. "I know, Sybil. I'll take her to the stand with me. She loves being outside in the wagon." He stood to leave, then spoke again. "Maybe tonight, after she's asleep, I can teach you some signs Emma is teaching me. Lyddie seems to understand them, even trying to use the easy ones, like *more* and *please.*"

"Not tonight. I plan to wash my hair and do my nails," Sybil said as she left the bedroom.

He stared at the door and shook his head. Since his visit to the specialist, Sybil's behavior toward her daughter changed. She took care of her mechanically, meeting her needs, but not mothering her. She never played with her as she had in the past and she never talked about her future.

How can I get her to accept Lyddie as a child who's deaf?

Will scanned the sky as he took his produce to the stand. Already the end of August and there hadn't been any significant rain since the end of June—only a few thundershowers which passed so quick, the ground barely soaked in needed water. Today he only had some okra, a few bunches of greens, and some rhubarb.

A glance at the sky revealed a few dark clouds building in the west. He offered a quick prayer. *God, a good rain would get the potatoes ready to pull. Those always sell well. Could you send those rain clouds our way today? And while you're at it, send someone to buy this rhubarb. I'm not sure how to cook it, and I know Sybil won't know.*

He looked over at Lyddie, sitting in the red wagon, chewing on a teething toy. When she saw her daddy, she offered him a smile, showing off her two little teeth. He bent down and signed the word *daddy*. A father's pride welled up in him as she swatted her forehead in a poor imitation of the sign.

"That's okay, lil' darlin'. You'll get the hang of it soon enough," Will whispered before he planted a big kiss on her forehead.

The sound of screeching tires drew him to his feet. That noise only came from Matilda Stotler's driving. He'd heard it often this summer as she'd visited his produce stand at least once a week.

"Good morning, Will," she said as she heaved herself out of the car. He suppressed a laugh at the sight of her dress, which fit tight around her large girth. Her outfit, though obviously expensive, was at least two sizes too small. She wore a yellow summer hat large enough to double as an umbrella. Her bright red hair, with sprinkles of gray, seemed reluctant to stay within the confines of her hairpins.

"It's going to be a hot one, isn't it? But I see those clouds. Maybe we'll get rain before you know it. Now what do you have for sale today, and where is that baby girl?"

"Morning, Mrs. Stotler. I'm hoping that rain's coming. If it does, I'll have some potatoes in about two weeks. Lyddie is right here in her wagon."

The older woman made her way to the baby. "Well, hello, little miss. I'm glad to see you're out here helping your daddy today. I think he can use some customers and you're just the sweet thing to draw them in."

Lyddie stared at the lady with her huge blue eyes and slowly rewarded her with a smile.

"I do believe she is the prettiest baby I've ever seen." Matilda said, as she rummaged through her huge purse. "I brought her something. Well, it's more for you and Sybil than for her. It's a book about sign language. Shows you all the ways to make the letters and the words. I ordered it from the school for the deaf in Romney."

He stiffened. "Mrs. Stotler, I've already told..."

"Don't get your dander up, Will. I know you don't want to send her there. I don't want her to go either." She thumped on the cover of the book. "If you plan to keep her here, then learn this. It's only right to do your best for her. Now, what do you have from that wonderful garden of yours? Rhubarb! Oh, my gracious! I'll have pies baked by sundown."

He held the book in his hands and swallowed hard, trying to keep the tears he felt pooled behind his eyes from coming forward as Matilda rolled away. She bought all of his rhubarb and a good amount of greens and okra. He knew she couldn't possibly eat so much and suspected she passed it on to the soup kitchen at her church.

Matilda had become not only a good customer, but a good friend. She always listened, and never minced her words. She was straightforward, tough on the exterior with insides as soft as yeast dough. *I understand now why mother liked her.*

Since he'd stood at her door when he first met her, she'd made it a point to come visit them. She was loving with Lyddie and often drew Will into a conversation about apple farming or the Depression. She freely gave her opinions, but listened to him in return.

Her way with Sybil impressed him the most. She used an outspoken yet motherly way to which Sybil responded well. She'd spent one entire morning carefully instructing Sybil how to make biscuits and gravy while sprinkling her conversation with words of wisdom about caring for children.

Will watched as she left the stand, driving as erratically as ever. He knew full well she could have sent her maid to buy the produce or even bought from one of the truck farmers on the square. Instead she came here and Will thanked God for her visits.

Two more trucks stopped and by noon he'd sold all his okra and most of the greens. The rest he'd take home to have with a pan of cornbread for their supper. Sybil fretted about the lack of meat, but they could only eat meat a few times a week now, as their budget wouldn't allow for more.

He held on to his hat when the wind suddenly came in gusts before they reached the farmhouse. A loud clap of thunder made Will look to see if the sound frightened Lyddie. Then he remembered.

Will I ever not forget she's deaf? The thought of all the sounds she'd never know saddened him.

He went to sleep that night with the tap of steady rain on the tin roof. Another sound his daughter wouldn't hear.

Chapter 23

*T*he rain persisted through the night and settled in for the next day. By mid-morning, he couldn't stay in the house any longer.

"Sybil, I'm going to town. I need to find a distributor for our apple crop and a crew to help harvest. This rain came at just the right time. If cooler temperatures follow it, the apples should be plentiful come October."

"The harvest?" Sybil glared at him from her place on the sofa with a shocked look on her face. "How can you even think of harvesting your apples this year? You know what long hours that takes. Who'll watch Lyddie? You'll just have to let your precious apples rot this year. I can't go through another harvest alone with Lyddie."

Anger coursed through Will. Not harvest the apples? *Over my dead body will I let my apples rot.*

He took a deep breath and hissed, "Without the

apple money, we've got nothing to live on through the winter!" He picked up his cap and started for the door. "I'll find a way to harvest the apples and you'll find a way to care for our daughter." He left before she could respond.

The drive to town crawled at a slow pace. Rain made the road slick and visibility poor. Will realized how foolish it had been to come out in this weather. Still, he kept going and used the time to talk to God.

"Lord, I know you mean to provide for us, and I don't want to get ahead of you. But I could never bear to see those apples rot on the ground. Not after so many generations of harvesting them. I need a distributor and a crew. Can you work it out for me, please? I trust you for this."

By the time he arrived in Berkley, the rain had slackened and he'd formalized a plan. He'd start at O'Bryan's Mercantile to see if Sean knew of any distributors, then he'd put a sign on the community bulletin board outside the post office asking for a harvesting crew.

Tom's truck sat in front of the diner, so Will stopped for a quick cup of coffee and a visit with his friend. Maybe this would be the time to talk with Tom about whatever he'd gotten himself into. Will swatted his cap on his right knee to get the rainwater off it and entered the diner's door, searching for Tom. He spotted him in the back booth, with Emma sitting across from him.

"Hey, you up for another cup of coffee?" he asked as he approached the booth.

Both Tom and Emma seemed flustered by Will's appearance.

"I have to get back to work," Emma said as she exited the booth without even a hello.

Tom ducked his head and mumbled, "Sure, but it'll have to be quick. I've got some place to go."

Will sat down across from Tom, and within moments, Emma brought two steaming cups of fresh coffee to the table. She offered Will a small nod and left immediately.

"Is everything all right? You and Emma seem—"

"We're fine. You know how women can be when they get a thought in their head." Tom offered a small grin, which Will thought looked more like a grimace.

"I wonder if you might be available to hire on for the harvest this fall. I can..."

Tom took a long swallow of his coffee and stood. "Sorry, I've got a good job, which I need to get to right now."

Will watched, stunned, as his friend left the diner. His concern for Tom ballooned.

Emma came back to the table. "I'm sorry, Will. I saw what happened. He doesn't mean to be rude. He has a lot on his shoulders right now." She sighed and gazed at the diner door as if she could make him return. When she turned back, she offered Will a small smile. "And add to that the fact that I'm not happy about what he's doing."

"Emma, tell me what he's doing. I want to help."

"No, it's for him to tell you. I reckon if he wanted you to know, he'd have already told you." She took a deep breath and continued. "Now, what brings you to town on such an awful day?"

"I need to find a distributor for my apples. Harvest will be here soon and since the Demarcos left, I need to find someone to sell them to. I'm headed over to O'Bryan's to ask Sean if he's heard anything from the other apple farmers."

Emma drummed her fingers on the tabletop, then said, "What a minute! I read something in the newspaper this morning. I think it might be what you're looking for." She rushed behind the counter and grabbed a newspaper. Back at the booth, she spread out the back page. "Read this advertisement."

Will read the short ad, shook his head as if he couldn't make sense of the words, then read it again, slower this time.

Wanted: fresh apples to sell to vendors on the streets of New York City. Distribution point will be the train station in Lewisburg every Monday morning, mid-September through November. Apple farmers can contact us at the address below. New York State Apple Distributors.

He looked at Emma, scarcely able to believe what he just read.

"It's true, Will. I read an article about how men, corporate men who lost their jobs when the stock market crashed, have formed a group to sell apples on the streets in their city. It'll help them and the farmers. Do you think you might distribute your apples to them?"

"I don't know. What if it's a scam? If they don't show at the train station, I'd be without a distributor."

"How can it be a scam if they aren't asking for money up front? At least write to them. I've got paper and an envelope behind the counter. The post goes out at two today."

In this moment, Will remembered his prayer. *Is this the answer?* Then he thought of the sales from yesterday's produce. The coins lay heavy in his front pants pocket. "I'll do better than that. I'll send a telegraph right now." Excited, he pushed up from his seat, then plopped back into the booth. "But I can't make a commitment with this company if I don't have pickers."

Emma drummed her fingers again, then snapped her right thumb and forefinger. "Turn back to the first page. I think you might find some pickers."

Confused but curious, he flipped the paper over. The headline read **Hooverville Established in Lewisburg**. He scanned the article, reading about the homeless families living in tents at the county fairgrounds. He'd heard about these tent cities but didn't know one was so close. He thought they were all in the Midwest where the dust bowl scavenged the land.

"I don't know, Emma. Do you think they'd be reliable, and even more important, honest?" He thought of Sybil and Lyddie Anne and their safety.

"You know as well as I do, Will Parson," she said as she thumped the newspaper with her forefinger, "these people are good, hardworking folks, down on their luck. They're farmers and miners, just like us. Only difference is, by God's grace, we still have our homes."

Will's face turned red, embarrassed by his qualms and fears. Who was he to doubt? "Thank you, Emma. You're an answer to a very recent prayer."

Chapter 24

*A*s Will dug the last of his potatoes, he heard
Matilda's car coming down his drive at a high
speed. "Lord, let her find the brakes before she runs
into my house." A hand across the forehead shaded
him from the sun as he watched the vehicle come to a
screeching stop when she spotted in him in the field.

She got out of the car with a speed which alarmed
him. He let his hoe drop to the ground and sprinted
toward her.

"Mrs. Stotler, what's wrong? Has something
happened?" That's when he saw an envelope in
her hand—a yellow one, which could only mean a
telegram. Who would send him a telegram?

"Since I'm not in the habit of reading other
people's communications, I'm sure I don't know. But
it's a telegram, so I thought it might be important."
She handed over the envelope and waited.

He held it in his hands for a moment, then opened it with one swift tear.

Received inquiry about apple crop Stop Interested in becoming your distributor Stop Meeting for all apple farmers at city hall in Lewisburg next Tuesday 10AM Stop New York City Apple Company Stop

"Thank you, God. Hallelujah!" he shouted as he grabbed Matilda and gave her a big bear hug.

"My goodness. Have you lost your senses? Let go of me and tell me what this obviously good news is."

"I'm back in business. I have a distributor for this year's apple crop. My apples are going to be sold on the streets of New York City. Isn't that something?"

"Then I'm glad I went to Western Union to send a telegram and cajoled Homer into letting me bring this one to you this morning. Fool man. He planned to wait until his son brought lunch, then let him deliver it with a few others."

She straightened her bodice and her hat, both of which became dislodged when he almost lifted her off her feet from the hug. "I know that boy. Not enough brains in his head to fill a teacup. No telling when you'd have gotten the message."

"I'm sure glad you did, Mrs. Stotler. It's the best news I've had in years."

"Here's another piece of news for you. From now on, call me Matilda, not Mrs. Stotler. Anybody who gives me hugs should be on a first name basis."

"Yes, ma'am, Mrs. Stol... I mean, Matilda. You're a good friend and I thank God for you."

"Oh, go on with you! Now get those potatoes dug. I'll be by tomorrow for two bushels, so make sure you save some for me." She got into her vehicle and removed a hankie from her pocket to wipe her eyes.

Will watched as his already full heart overflowed. "Lord, you're so good to send us Matilda. Now, please help me find a crew, and help Sybil accept the news that there will indeed be a harvest."

A crispness in the cool morning air gave promise to the end of summer's heat. Will loved autumn in the mountains, when the leaves turned to rich splashes of color and his apples went from green to bright red. He had a lightness he'd not felt in months. Even if he didn't get what he wanted for his apples, he'd be working again. It made him think of Tom. He understood a man's need to work.

He stopped at Matilda's, where she made him stay for a breakfast so large it made his eyes bulge—eggs, bacon and sausage, fluffy hot biscuits, and blueberry pancakes. Will wanted to ask her if she ate like this every day. She must, since she hadn't known he'd visit. He left with a full stomach and a glad heart. Matilda promised to visit Sybil and Lyddie while he took care of his business.

The drive to Lewisburg took longer than usual. His truck plodded along behind a milk wagon that struggled with the inclines and curves on the mountainous road. With no way to pass, he crawled at a ridiculous speed for many miles. Frustrated, Will laid down on his horn, then felt an immediate reprimand in his spirit. Embarrassed by his behavior, he slowed his pace even more and backed off the bumper of the wagon.

"Okay, Lord. Let's do this on your time. Help me with my impatience."

Finally, he came to the city limits of Lewisburg and followed the signs to the fairgrounds. When he arrived, he slowed to a stop, then pulled to the side of the road. The few pictures in newspapers didn't prepare him for his first site of a shantytown.

Before him were maybe a hundred shanties constructed of cardboard, tar paper, glass, lumber, and tin—whatever materials the residents could salvage. The make-do homes crowded together like peas in a pod, with only narrow walking spaces between. Children ran barefoot and played with sticks and other scavenged items. Men huddled together, some talking, others just sitting.

Will left his truck parked where it stood and walked on the narrow road, which wound through the camp. Just a few steps in, he became aware of something more than the lack of a decent place to sleep or adequate clothes. A heavy blanket of hopelessness shrouded the place. The women methodically washed clothes or cooked on small fires outside their shanty with barely a smile, dragging their feet, and only halfway reprimanding their rowdy kids. The men had eyes either dull or filled with anger. Will avoided looking directly at them.

He'd walked only a few yards when he realized children followed him. When he stopped and turned around, they stopped as well. One, the apparent leader, stepped forward and asked, "Hey, mister. You got any food?"

His heart dropped. What could he say to these children? Never in his life had he been hungry enough to ask a stranger for food. The bountiful breakfast he'd eaten soured in his stomach. He silently shook his head and continued walking, with the hope they wouldn't follow.

A few steps later he stopped in the middle of the road and prayed. *Lord, I believe it's your plan to send me here to find someone to work the harvest. Now I need you to guide my feet to those people.* Before he lifted his head, he heard a soft voice calling his name—a voice he recognized. When he looked up, he saw Eleanor standing in front of a tent with a bundle of wet clothes in her hands.

"Will, I can't believe you're here. It's so good to see you." She placed the wet clothes on a piece of cardboard lying on the ground next to her wash pot and waited for him to walk over.

He hesitated, not sure what had happened. He didn't want to see Eleanor's family living like this. Then he remembered his prayer. *Surely, it's not Eleanor and Carl I'm here to hire. How can I? Carl has too much pride and I still remember how he rejected me in his office.*

Forgive and love your neighbor. The words came through clearly, as though someone had spoken into his ear. Will knew instantly the words spoken in his heart were from God.

He walked to Eleanor and put out his hand for a shake. "Hello, Eleanor," he said, as his eyes roamed for Carl. "How... what...?"

"You're surprised. I am too, every morning when I wake up in this tent and realize it's my home. But we're okay. We have more than most around us, so I'm grateful."

Will stared at this amazing woman, not sure what to say next. Eleanor's willingness to share their story met his silence.

"We were in the hotel in Romney, looking for a house to rent. We found a place, nothing fancy, but it was in the country with plenty of room for the three of us. We planned to move into it at the end of the week. Then Johnny found us, and before supper Carl had given him all our funds for his promise to return before the weekend with triple the amount." She paused with a deep sigh, then continued.

"Of course he never returned, and we couldn't pay rent for the house or the motel bill. We had to leave, and this is our only option. The motel owner kindly gave us this old tent, which I'm grateful for when I look around at what others here have.

"Danny and I have adapted, but it's been hard on Carl. His pride is hurt, and now he knows Johnny's a con artist. He spends his day sitting at one of the gates, holding an empty pipe in his mouth—no money for tobacco." She paused and gave a small laugh. "Listen to me. I'm rattling on about us and haven't even asked about you and your family."

Will found his voice and replied, "We're fine. Lyddie Anne is growing like a weed. I do have sad news about her. She can't hear. Profoundly deaf, the specialist in Charleston said." It embarrassed him to share his troubles when she'd obviously been through much tougher times recently.

"I'm so sorry. She's such a precious baby. But I know she's bright. I could see it in her eyes. She'll do well. How's Sybil?"

He hesitated. How could he tell her about Sybil

in light of what she was living through? He finally replied, "She's trying to handle everything."

A silence stretched between them, making him uncomfortable.

"Are you going to share with me why you're here in our Hooverville today? I suspect it's not a sightseeing tour." Eleanor stood with her head tilted to one side.

Before responding, he offered a quick prayer. *It's in your hands, Lord. Give me the words to say.*

"I came here looking for a crew to help me with the apple harvest. I've found a distributor, but I need help with the harvest." He stopped, not sure what to say next. Eleanor's face fill with joy.

"Are you asking Carl and me to work in your orchard? You'd give us work after the way Carl treated you?" Her eyes searched his.

"Truth is, Eleanor, I've listened to God more lately. He sent me here as an answer to my prayer to find a crew. Just now, while standing in the road, he told me to ask you and Carl." Will smiled and stretched out his hand for a shake. "So I'm asking and I hope you'll say yes. I have a foreman's cottage for you to live in. It's not much, but I reckon it's a more solid roof than this one." He jerked his other arm toward the tent behind Eleanor.

"Oh, thank God for you." She took his hand and covered it with both of hers. "I'm not sure how good of workers we'll be with Carl's limp and Danny's wandering, but I promise we'll try our best. I'll get Carl there, even if I have to tie him up in this tent and drag him there!"

They spoke for a few minutes longer, making plans for when they should come and how long the harvest would last. "If the harvest is good, and I believe it will be, maybe you can stay on and help with the farm—at least through the next harvest."

When he turned to retrace his steps back to his truck, he heard Danny screaming his name. "Mr. Will, Mr. Will! You come!" He almost knocked Will over in his excitement to shake his hand.

"I sure did, Danny. And now you're coming to visit me."

Danny grabbed him in a big hug before he stepped back and announced, "It 'someday' now, huh, Mr. Will?"

Will laughed, amazed at Danny's memory. He waved and started for his truck.

At the entrance of the Hooverville, a tall gaunt man stepped up to him. "Mister, can you spare a dime?" Will looked at the young face and dug deep into his pocket for a dime.

Chapter 25

*D*anny jumped from the back of the truck before it had rolled to a stop. "Mama, Will's house!" He pointed to the large farmhouse just up the drive from the foreman's cottage.

"Yes, son, I see." She stood and moved to the end of the truck. "Now give me a hand so I can get down."

On the ground, she put her hands on her back and stretched. It had been a long bumpy ride from Lewisburg in the back of Will's truck, with Danny's constant chatter and unbridled happiness. Unlike inside the truck, where Will and Carl drove in what must have been an uncomfortable silence between them.

She surveyed the outside of the cottage, instantly taken back to her family home in Pineville. She hoped this home would be filled with as much love as the home she'd grown up in. It would take a miracle, since Carl still resisted the idea of being Will's employee.

She didn't know how much labor he'd be willing to do. And, if he didn't, would Will let them stay?

She'd take things a day at a time. Gratitude filled her as she whispered, "Thank you, Lord, for providing this. Please let us be up to this task."

"Like I said, it's not much, but the roof doesn't leak and it's warm in the winter," Will said as he came around from the driver's side to stare at the cottage with Eleanor.

"It's fine. So much like the home I grew up in," she said as she began pulling baskets full of household items from the truck. "Carl, you take these baskets. Danny, you can help me with the boxes."

Will stepped up to pull a box from the bed, but Eleanor put her hand on his arm. "No, you've already lost almost a day's work. You go do your chores. The three of us can handle this."

He hesitated, then glanced at Carl and back to Eleanor. "If you're sure, I'll go check on Sybil and the baby." He gave one last glance at Carl, who had yet to lift any baskets, then got into his truck. He turned the key over only to hear a short sputter, then nothing. Will shook his head and tried again. Nothing. He spoke to Eleanor out his open window. "Tank's empty. I didn't want to stop in town for gas because..."

She nodded. How like him to think of their feelings. He knew it would embarrass Carl to have the Rhode family hauled around by Will with their few possessions in his truck. The town would know soon enough, but she breathed a sigh of relief, grateful they'd been spared the spread of the news for now.

"I'll leave it here until morning. I have gasoline in

the tractor to siphon out. Should be enough to get me back to Berkley."

In short order, their few possessions were unpacked and in place. She saw Carl pull something from his clothing sack and slipp it into his deep pants pocket. "I'm going to walk a bit. I'm stiff from the truck ride," he announced, and turned away without waiting for her reply.

Eleanor watched him leave, suspicious of what he put in his pocket, but decided not to confront him. It would be best to let him work out his feelings about being here. At least he had come—something she'd feared might not happen.

"Mama, I go see Mr. Will in apple house. I help him." Danny said, expectantly.

Her heart melted. He'd had so little to do in the shantytown and had been the recipient of teasing more than once. "Okay, Danny. But try not to get in his way. And come home before dark. I'll make some soup from the meat Will gave us."

Eleanor savored her time alone in the cottage, thrilled to be in a home instead of a tent. She hummed as she wiped down the shelves above the sink, where she planned to put their few dishes. A pie safe and a Hoosier cabinet sat to the right of the sink. The opposite wall held a stove and a small icebox. Tears flooded her eyes when she opened the ice box filled with butter, milk, eggs, and bacon. She'd had enough oatmeal to last her a lifetime. Tomorrow morning, she'd make fluffy biscuits with eggs and bacon. Bless Will Parson.

Once the kitchen sparkled to her approval, she peeled potatoes for the soup. Her mind wandered to the last few days spent in Hooverville. It had not been easy to convince Carl to come to Applewood Orchard, let alone work for Will. He fussed and fumed, but in the end, he'd crawled into the truck. She only hoped his limp leg wouldn't hamper his work. She didn't think she could bear having to move back to life in a tent again.

Eleanor had the soup simmering on the stove when she noticed the kitchen had grown dark. She stepped out the door and heard a noise. She turned to greet Danny, wondering why he came from a direction opposite of the apple house. Carl came toward the house, not Danny. And he stumbled in a telltale way she knew all too well.

Her heart sank as she realized what he'd put into his pocket. He must have bartered for some moonshine whiskey before they left the shantytown. Goodness knows plenty of bootlegging went on among the men there. Mostly homemade, not the good stuff Carl had before their circumstances changed.

What he'd bartered with, she didn't know. But it would be best if Will didn't see him in this state. Eleanor rushed to meet him and caught him just before he stumbled over a large rock. With one arm around his waist, she hooked an arm over her shoulder and got him inside to the bed. He passed out just as a loud clap of thunder hit her ears. "Danny!" she whirled around and raced out the door toward the apple house.

Danny feared two things—the dark and thunder. Frantic to find him, she hoped to get her son home before the storm hit. But the heavy rain began as she reached the door of the apple house.

"Danny, it's time to come ho..." Eleanor stopped

when she saw no one was about. Her heart thumped in her chest as she tried to think. Could he be at Will's house? Surely not for this long. She ran toward the house, ignoring the pounding rain.

Her muddy shoes made her almost slip as she rushed onto the porch. Regaining her balance, she pounded hard on the door, afraid the loud storm would prevent anyone from hearing her frantic knock.

Sybil opened the door and blinked when she saw a soaked Eleanor standing there. "Why, Eleanor. Why are you out in this rain?" She didn't give her a chance to respond before she broke into a sob. "Oh, Eleanor, Lyddie Anne is deaf. Did you know? I can't possibly care for a deaf child. Will said we won't send her..."

"We'll talk about this later. Right now, I need to get Danny home. He doesn't like storms," she interrupted, too alarmed to listen to Sybil's troubles.

"Danny? He's not here. I haven't seen him. Will got back from the orchard just before the storm broke. He's upstairs, cleaning up."

An icy chill traveled through Eleanor's body. Not here? Where could he be? Then it hit her.

He's gone back to the estate. He must think Sam and the horses are back.

She braced herself on the door frame and forced her words. "Can you get Will, please? I need help. Danny's missing."

"I'm here, Eleanor." Will rushed down the stairs and came to stand in front of the door.

"I let Danny go to the apple house hours ago. He said you were there. I thought he saw you going in." The sob she'd been holding back escaped. "Oh, I don't know where he is, and he's very frightened of storms.

Wherever he is, he'll be hiding until this storm is over. Please help me find him."

"Let me pull on some boots and get my jacket. We can't use the truck; we'll have to walk. You go back and get into something dry and bring Carl. Together, I'm sure we'll find him nearby."

"Carl can't help."

Will's look told her she needed to be honest. To hide things from their new employer would never do. "I'm sorry. He must have bartered for some moonshine before we left. He's been upset about coming. He went for a walk right after you left us. I got him back just before he passed out." She paused, then continued when Will remained silent. "It won't happen again. I promise. There's no place here to get the stuff."

"Let's discuss this later. Right now, we need to find Danny." Will glanced at his wife. "Sybil, take Eleanor upstairs and get her some dry clothes. Make sure they're warm. The sun will set soon, and it'll get a lot colder if this rain keeps up. I'll get a couple of lanterns and slickers from the barn."

Before Eleanor went to change, she said, "I think he might have tried to go back to the estate. He's still so upset about the horses and Sam. Maybe he thinks they're back."

Will nodded. "Hurry and change. We need to use all the daylight we can."

Within ten minutes, they headed toward the orchard. "We'll go through here. It's the shortest way to the estate." Another clap of thunder hurried their steps.

Eleanor prayed as she walked through the blinding rain. "Lord, please let him have gotten to the estate before the storm hit. Please keep him there until we can get to him."

The fifteen-minute walk to the estate took almost thirty in the bad weather. Will stopped just outside the fence to light the lanterns. "We'll need light inside the house. Do you know a way to get in?"

"No, but if Danny got in, I think we can as well." She watched as he worked with the lanterns, willing his hands to move faster.

At the estate, they walked around the huge porch as they called Danny's name. When they got no answer, Will pulled on the large windows, but they were all locked.

"I'll need to break one open to get inside, Eleanor. But since he hasn't answered, I'm not sure he's in there. I don't see any evidence of him getting in. It's your choice."

Every particle in Eleanor's body wanted to break the door down or break all the windows out—anything to find her son. But she knew Will was correct. Danny would never think to break into a place. If he got here, he'd be crouched on the porch. "No, he's not here. We need to check the stables." She headed toward them without waiting for a response.

"Danny, are you here? Talk to me, son. I know you're scared. But Mr. Will and I are here to take you home. Answer me now, Danny!" Eleanor kept repeating her words as they searched the stables until Will touched her lightly on the arm.

"He's not here, Eleanor. We need to go back to the house and call the sheriff. Just pray this storm hasn't knocked out the phone lines."

Fear assaulted her as the fact Danny wasn't here

settled in her mind and her knees buckled. Will caught her before she hit the stable floor. He helped her to a square bale of hay.

"Sit a minute, Eleanor. Then we'll start back. Who knows, maybe we'll find him in the orchard or maybe he'll be back at the house playing with Lyddie and making Sybil nuts with all his chatter." Will tried to give her some hope.

His words were lost on her, but she tried to be brave. "Okay, let's start back then. He'll be cold and hungry when we find him."

The rain slowed by the time they reached the orchard. They moved as fast as the slippery ground allowed. She took the lead, with Will behind her. They repeated Danny's name, often with a sob from her. Eleanor held her lantern high when she saw something to her left. "Danny!" she yelled as she raced toward it, stumbling over an apple tree root. She caught her fall on a nearby tree and hurried on with Will close behind.

There, hung from a low branch of an apple tree, she saw Danny's cap. This time, it wasn't a root that made her fall. Her knees simply gave way. "Oh, Danny. Where are you?"

Chapter 26

*T*illy put another piece of wood in her stove and
filled a pot with water. She looked forward to a
big bowl of grits and a slice of fresh bread made this
morning. She moved to her table to slice the bread
when a flash of lightning drew her eyes to the window.

Fear crawled up her spine. Was someone out
there? When the clap of thunder came, she heard
someone cry out.

"Lord, someone's out there," she whispered,
terrified. Tilly grabbed the knife she always kept
beside her bed as she prayed. "God, I been readin'
that you're always with us. Be with me now and keep
me safe. I sure don't want to use this knife. Help me
know what to do." Peace followed. Her shaking hands
grew still, and she took a deep breath when she heard
crying. "Whoever it is, I don't reckon there's danger."
Still, she kept the knife with her as she moved out the
door.

She waited a moment, not able to see through the darkness. Then a bright bolt of lightning allowed her to scan the land around the cabin. There! Someone huddled in a tight ball at the edge of the meadow. Should she approach? Was it safe?

A clap of thunder followed by a pitiful sound set her feet into motion, and she sprinted toward the scream. She stopped when she saw a grown man huddled beneath a large oak tree, his arms wrapped around his head.

Unsure of how to approach him, she spoke before she went any closer. "Mister, you all right?"

The screaming stopped, but the man didn't move. "You hurt? Can I help? I have medicines."

Still no response, only sobs. She took small steps toward him. What if she was about to step into a trap?

"I want Mama. Please. Afraid."

Mama? This might be a grown man, but he acted like a child. Her mother's heart spoke, and she moved closer. "It's a terrible storm, but it'll pass soon. I reckon God's protecting us right now."

The man lifted his head then and hiccuped before responding. "That's what Mama says."

Tilly recognized him then, more from his voice than the shadowy view of his face. He used to ride in the arena at the big house. How did he get here?

"Danny?" she said as she stepped closer. "Are you Danny?"

"Yes. I want my mama."

"Well, we can't find her until this storm is over. Come to my cabin so you can get dry. You'll be safe there." She waited. What would she do if he refused?

But he slowly stood up and took a step closer. "I'm hungry."

"Well, I guess I can take care of that, if you like grits and bread."

"I like grits with honey." Another flash of lightning caused him to crouch, ready to scream.

Tilly spoke quickly. "It's okay. The lightning's farther away. The storm's almost over. Come on. It's just a short walk to my cabin."

Relieved when he followed her, she walked quickly before another lightning strike could frighten him again. They arrived at the cabin within minutes.

"Come on in. If you want to get out of that wet shirt, I have a dry one. Don't think my pants will fit. You're a pretty big man."

"Mama says I a big boy." Danny smiled, visually relaxing. "Oh." He backed up and pointed. "What's that?"

Tilly looked at the spot where he pointed. Solomon had crawled out from under her bed. "That's my turtle, Solomon. He doesn't like storms either. Reckon he was hiding under there."

Danny seemed to be thinking about what she said. Then he brightened. "If storm comes back, I hide there too."

"I don't think you'll need to. The rain has slowed, and I don't hear any thunder. Storm's 'bout over. I'll get you a towel and shirt."

Dried and wearing Tilly's shirt, Danny engaged in a long conversation with Solomon, sharing his fears caused by the storm. Tilly finished the grits and fixed a large bowl with a slice of bread. "Come sit in my chair at the table, Danny. You can eat now." Danny ate as she watched from her rocker. *What do I do with him now?*

Will grabbed Danny's cap and pulled Eleanor to her feet. "Be strong, Eleanor. I don't think he's in the orchard or we would've found him already. I think we should look in the woods. If he came this way, he's lost for sure. We need to keep moving toward him."

He headed into the forest near the beehives. Eleanor followed close behind. Thankfully, the lightning and thunder moved on, and the rain had lessened. He held the lantern close to the ground, hoping to find a track, then realized the rain had likely covered any footprints.

"Lord, show me the way." As soon as he whispered the words, he saw a path, so narrow it could be easy to miss.

This way. The soft words hit his thoughts and his heart at the same time.

He swung around to Eleanor and grabbed her arm. "I've found a path. It's not very wide, so stay close and watch your step."

"Do you think Danny went this way?"

"I don't know, but I think we should follow it."

She nodded and pulled her slicker tighter as she lifted the lantern. "I'll keep up."

The path turned out to be a pattern of zig-zags—to the right, then to the left. More than once, Will thought he'd lost the trail and found it again by turning in the opposite direction. He started a soft chant, "Right—left, right—left."

Another left turn and the path ended in a small

clearing. There, near the edge of the woods, sat a small cabin. Light shone through the single window; smoke curled from a stovepipe on the roof.

Eleanor spoke first. "Did you know someone lives in these woods?"

"I've wondered. We need to check it out. Danny could be in there."

Before he could say more, she broke into a run, headed for the cabin. "Danny! Are you in there?" She banged hard on the door.

"Mama!" The door opened wide as Danny rushed out. "You find me. I was scared."

Will watched the reunion between mother and son. Beyond them, in the glow of the single kerosene lamp, he saw small black woman dressed in men's clothing. Her eyes held the look of a deer about to flee from danger. He knew what he said and how he said it would be crucial.

"I'm Will Parson. This is Eleanor Rhode. I guess you've met Danny. Thank you for helping him."

Her response was slow to come. She grabbed a piece of wood from her stack near the stove. "Name's Tilly Sayre. Best come in. It's cold and wet out there." She pushed the small log onto the stove.

He marveled at her voice. It sounded almost musical and held notes of a dialect he'd not heard in years.

Once they were inside, she seemed embarrassed. "Don't reckon I can ask you to sit. I'm short of chairs."

Will shook his head. "No, we're fine standing, just happy to—"

"Reckon I should tell you what happened," she interrupted, holding one palm in the air. "I found

Danny out in the storm. He was scared, so I brought him here."

He knew she would say little else. Still, he wanted to know more about her.

"Miss... uh...Tilly, how long have you lived here?"

Unblinking brown eyes and silent lips met his question.

Eleanor stepped forward and extended her right hand. When Tilly hesitantly reach to shake it, she said, "Thank you for helping Danny. I'm very grateful." She glanced at the shirt Danny had on. "And thank you for giving him some dry clothes. I'll get the shirt back to you soon. You've been a blessing tonight."

She released Tilly's hand and turned to Danny. "Come on, son. We need to get home. Thank Miss Tilly for her hospitality."

"Thank you. The grits was good. I like Solomon."

Tilly nodded her head once.

Will knew it was best to leave. Fear never left the woman's eyes. As they walked past the table toward the door, his eyes landed on a half-empty jar of honey. His honey.

Chapter 27

*T*illy watched from the window as the three of them followed the path away from her cabin. Her world had gone off-kilter. She reached for the windowsill to steady herself. Danger had taken residence at her door, causing a familiar tightness in her chest.

Big Mama's words came to her as they often did when she became anxious. *If you get scared, just keep putting one foot in front of the other. Things have a way of working out.* This time, Tilly wasn't so sure.

She grabbed a dishtowel to cover the pot of grits and the bread, then moved to her rocker and opened her Bible. Unlike other evenings when the Word soothed her soul, it brought little comfort tonight. Long after midnight, she finally went to bed, only to dream of three people who walked her trail.

For the next few days, Tilly stayed close to the cabin where she could scan the meadow, watchful of more visitors. On the third day, she heard footsteps.

Before she could exit the work shed, Eleanor entered, her arms full.

"Hello, Tilly. I brought your shirt back. And a fresh apple pie." She held out the pie and continued, "I thought we could share a piece with a hot cup of coffee."

Share? Tilly's mind scrambled to find the meaning of the word. To share something, there had to be someone to share with. A companion. Slowly, like the spring thaw of a frozen river, the hard shell around her heart cracked and fell away. Within her arose a deep longing—a desire to visit with another woman. She nodded her head in agreement.

"Reckon I could use a cup."

Eleanor smiled and moved back to allow her to pass. Inside the cabin, Tilly put coffee grounds in the coffeepot, then filled a pot with water and put it on the stove. She placed her cup on the small table and rummaged through the shelf above the sink, searching for the other cup.

Once found, she held the cup in both hands as an icy fist of sadness gripped her heart. How many times had she filled this for Big Mama? The last time they visited, she should have noticed her grandmother's labored breathing and slow movements. Instead, caught up with herself, she complained of her loneliness. Big Mama died the next week.

"Tilly," Eleanor spoke in a soft voice. "The water's boiling."

Startled, Tilly lifted her head. She set the coffee cup on the table and moved to the pot of boiling water. "You're welcome to sit in the chair. I'll sit in my rocker."

Coffee poured and pie cut, the two women ate

in silence. It occurred to Tilly that she should speak, but she'd long ago lost the art of conversation. Staring down at the half-eaten slice of pie, she pushed words from her voice. "I'm thankin' you for this. Reckon it's been a long time since I had such a treat."

"Tilly, can you look at me, please?" Eleanor waited until a pair of brown eyes met hers. "You don't need to be afraid. I've talked with Will. We mean you no harm. We both want to be your friend."

But you don't know what... the thought came so strong, Tilly wondered if she spoke it out loud.

"Now." Eleanor got up and filled both their cups with fresh coffee. "Tell me about the plants I saw in your shed. I'm fascinated."

Relief coursed through Tilly. This she could talk about. As she shared her work with the plants, another forgotten emotion emerged within her. Hope grew with each word spoken.

Will fell into bed and slipped into his weariness like he'd slide into a warm bath. He and the Rhodes had spent the last three days working in the orchard getting things ready for the harvest. Eleanor and Danny picked up fallen limbs, stacking them in a pile to be burned. He and Carl used scythes to cut the high brush around the trees. Carl needed to stop often for a rest, but his effort impressed Will.

Since the night Carl lay passed out while Will and Eleanor searched for Danny, he hadn't drunk again. And he did whatever his employer bid of him. Now the orchard lay ready for the harvest to begin. Will explained the process to Eleanor and Carl, who listened attentively and asked appropriate questions. Danny loved the apple house and talked constantly about getting the apples from the trees.

Will's confidence grew. Between himself and his three workers, they could get the harvest done, although he'd feel better if he had at least one more. He left these thoughts for later and fell into a heavy sleep minutes after his head hit the pillow.

Loud barks jerked him from his sleep just after midnight. He swung his legs over the edge of the bed. "Daisy girl, this had better be real danger. I need my sleep." He muttered quietly so as not to wake Sybil. Standing, he pulled on his pants and pushed his feet into the boots beside his bed.

At the bedroom door, he heard the barking again, only it wasn't coming from outside. It was coming from Lyddie's room.

He rushed to her room and found her struggling for breath between the rattling coughs, her eyes wide with fear. "What's wrong?" He lifted her to his shoulder, patting frantically on her back. "Lyddie Anne, it's Daddy. What happened? You were fine when I put you to bed."

Another string of hard coughing sent him running back to his bedroom. "Sybil, wake up! Something's wrong with the baby." When Sybil only moaned, he thought of Eleanor. Will grabbed a quilt from the end of the bed and threw it over Lyddie as he raced out of the house.

Holding Lyddie with one hand, he banged on the cottage's front door. "Eleanor, please let me in. I need your help." He waited for what seemed a long time, listening to the baby's labored breathing. The door opened just as he lifted his fist to knock again. Eleanor stood there, tying the belt to her robe. "Will, what's wrong?"

"It's Lyddie. She's sick. I don't know what to do."

She took the coughing baby in her arms, then turned frightened eyes to Will. "It's the croup. I've seen it before."

"Is it bad?" His heart skipped a beat.

"It can be. She needs medicine, but there's no time to get a doctor here. We must help with her breathing. You need to get Tilly."

Will blinked, confused. "Why Tilly?"

"Because I saw all the medicines she makes from plants. She'll know what we need. I'll take Lyddie back to your kitchen and wait there. Make sure you tell Tilly she has a barking cough and can't breathe. Hurry now. She needs help soon."

Will looked at Lyddie for another moment and left the cottage in a sprint.

Chapter 28

*T*illy's feet hit the floor as her hand reached for the ever-present knife. She stood frozen, watching the cabin door rattle with each hard pound.

"Tilly! Tilly, please open the door. My baby needs you." The voice, riddled with panic, was unrecognizable. In a softer voice she heard, "It's me, Will Parson. I need your help. My baby is sick."

A baby? A baby needed her. Still, she couldn't move—fear cemented her feet to the floor. She heard another male's voice in her head. *There're six new kittens in the shed. You can have the pick of the liter.*

Another hard pound jerked her from the memory. She shook her head and tried to concentrate. Someone needed her. Then everything fell into place. *It's Will. His baby is sick.* Her inner self heard the whispered words, *Fear not.* She took a deep breath and moved to the door, holding the knife in the folds of her nightdress. Cracking the door only a few inches, she could make out Will's features and see the panic in his face.

Tilly opened the door wider and motioned for him to enter, then placed the knife by the sink without turning her eyes from Will. She stood still, waiting.

"It's the baby. She woke up with a bad cough. She can hardly breathe. It's the croup. Eleanor sent me to get you." Will clinched and unclenched his hands, his words choppy, his breath labored. "Please come help. Eleanor says there's not time to get a doctor."

Seconds passed in silence. She heard another whispered word. *Trust.* After a deep inhale, Tilly spoke for the first time since Will entered the cabin. "I'll come. You head back now. Start lots of water to boilin'. Take the baby outside 'til I get there. Be easier for her to breathe in the night air." She moved to open the door for Will. "I'll get dressed and fetch my medicines. Won't be far behind you."

Tilly followed the trail from memory, her legs swift to move through the undergrowth. At the end of the woods, she stopped. Could she leave the woods after so many years? Then Will's words came to her. *My baby needs you.* The phrase propelled her feet forward.

Will had done exactly as she asked. When she arrived, he held Lyddie on the front porch. Tilly paused in front of him long enough to hear the labored breathing, then a series of coughs. Her heart squeezed tight. *Lord, this baby needs your help and so do I. Help me now, please.* Silent prayer over, she spoke to Will as she headed inside. "Bring her in now. We need to work fast."

In the kitchen, Eleanor had two large pots of

water boiling. Tilly gave her a nod and flew into action as she spoke. "Get these two chairs facing each other. I need a large, heavy quilt over them." She placed her basket on the counter and removed ground lobelia and mint. Using her cupped hand to measure, she threw a handful of the lobelia to both boiling pots.

When she turned, Eleanor had made a tent with the chairs and the quilt. Will stood near the table, holding the struggling baby.

Tilly stared at both of them and explained her plan. "I'll take the baby in my arms and crawl in there. Mr. Will, you take this pot of water and place it on the floor by us." She took Lyddie from him.

"Miz Eleanor, take the mint and soak it in hot water. Then squeeze the water out of it and wrap it in a dish towel. We need a poultice for her chest. Will, make sure plenty of water stays boilin'."

She took the baby and slipped into the homemade tent. When the poultice was ready, Eleanor reached under the quilt to hand it to her. Tilly laid it across Lyddie's chest and rocked her, back and forth, back and forth, as the air inside the tent filled with the smell of lobelia from the steaming water.

The three waited for what seemed like an eternity. They changed the steaming pots with the lobelia three times. After two hours under the tent, Lyddie's breathing became smoother and the coughing stopped. She fell into a peaceful sleep in Tilly's arms. She stayed under the tent for several more minutes, reveling at the feel of a baby in her arms.

"Mr. Will, you can take the quilt off now. I think she's gonna be okay."

Will and Eleanor removed the quilt and helped

Tilly to her feet. She handed the sleeping child to her father. "Her clothes are wet from the steam but it's best to let her sleep." Her own hair shone from droplets of water, her clothes drenched. She moved to the counter to collect her things.

"How can we ever thank you? I... you..." Will held Lyddie tight in his arms as he fought keep his voice from breaking. Unshed tears flooded his eyes.

Eleanor spoke up. "We're so thankful you came, Tilly. You've been a godsend tonight."

Tilly opened her mouth to speak just as Sybil entered the kitchen. "Will! What on earth is going on? Why is Eleanor here?" Her gazed moved to Tilly, then back to Will. "And who's this?"

"This is Tilly Sayre. She's our neighbor. Tilly saved our baby's life tonight. If she hadn't been here..." He dropped his face into the sleeping baby's chest, unable to say more.

"Lyddie can't possibly be sick. She was fine when we put her to bed." She glared at all three of them. "What's really going on here? This is my home, my kitchen, and my child. I demand to know."

Will's head popped up, his eyes blazing. He took a step toward his wife when Eleanor stopped him with her hand. "I'm going to walk Tilly part of the way back. Why don't you explain everything to Sybil?"

She turned to Tilly, who stood rooted next to the counter, eyes downcast. "Let's go, Tilly. You must be exhausted. We'll keep you updated on Lyddie's condition." She opened the kitchen door and waited for her to walk through it. Both women left without another word.

Tilly's heart hammered in her chest. *When Will tells her about my medicines, she'll know I'm the plant lady. He made a cross for every baby. Bet he don't know they was abortions 'stead of miscarriages. What if he finds out the truth? He'll probably blame me.* Her mind spun so fast she didn't realize they were at the path until she heard Eleanor talking.

"Thank you again, Tilly. Don't mind Sybil. She doesn't like surprises. She'll understand when Will explains it all to her. And she'll be grateful."

Tilly nodded, not sure that would be the case. She started down the path alone. Now another person knew of her existence. But as she walked, she remembered rocking the sweet baby and how it filled an emptiness within her. Then she did something she rarely did. She cried.

She spent the rest of the night in her rocker. Sleep evaded her. Never had she felt so vulnerable. Yet, each time she remembered the baby's peaceful sleep after the terrible gasping and coughing, she was glad she had gone.

She finally bowed her head in prayer. "Lord, what I've feared all these years has happened. This family knows I'm here, and before long they'll know I gave the wife cohosh—more than once. Forgive me for keeping those babies from being born. I'm ashamed and sorry."

At daybreak, she stoked her fire, made coffee, and took her cup outside in the morning mist. Her mind shot questions at her faster than she could process them. Should she leave the forest? Where would she go? Should she tell Will what she'd done? What would he do?

A doe walked to the edge of the clearing and grazed on the meadow grass. When Tilly moved her coffee cup to her lips, the deer jerked its head up, sensing danger. *It feels like I do—like danger is close.* She watched as it returned to grazing, satisfied the danger had passed. Time for her to do the same. She'd put one foot in front of the other and wait on God to direct her path.

She returned to the cabin for a quick breakfast, then grabbed her basket. She'd try again to collect more mushrooms, though doubtful she'd find any since the fall had been unseasonably dry. Still, she needed to do something.

Tilly spent the rest of the morning foraging with little to show for it by the time the sun stood high overhead. She continued her search, unwilling to stop her labor. She didn't want the questions to return.

When she finally lifted her eyes from the forest floor, she found herself near the big spruce by the beehives. Something large and brown sat at the edge of the woods. A bear? She came to an abrupt halt, ready to run. When it didn't move, she realized it wasn't a bear. She moved closer to find a high-back, four-legged brown chair.

In the seat, she found a note. *Thank you again. God bless you, Sybil and Will.* She gripped the paper in her hands and stared at the chair. Could it be they weren't angry with her? Was she truly safe with them? Then she had an unexpected thought—one that came with hope. She envisioned sitting at her table with Eleanor when—if—she came for another visit. It surprised her that she yearned for this very thing.

Chapter 29

*W*ill sat at the long table in the apple house, building wooden crates from thin pine slats. After the apples were picked and sorted, each crate would be filled. Then, he'd nail more slats across the top to ensure safe transport. Cutting each piece of wood to the exact measurement proved tedious. One wrong cut and the crate wouldn't go together properly, which had frustrated him more times than he could count.

He watched as Carl measured, then cut, then hammered with quiet confidence and impressive speed. It seemed to be a job he enjoyed, and Will was happy to let him take the lead. "Just tell me what you want me to do, Carl. I'm obliged to let you do the measuring."

Will noticed Carl stood a little straighter each time he praised him. He remembered his mother's words. *Everyone needs praise, son. Don't forget to give it often.* He marveled at God's grace as they worked in a quiet harmony he never thought would happen.

The morning passed quickly, and they finished eighteen crates by noon. "Carl, Will?" Eleanor's voice came from just beyond the apple house.

"Sounds like Eleanor's got your lunch ready, Carl. Why don't you..."

Eleanor appeared at the door, panic on her face. Will first thought of the baby. "Is Lyddie okay?"

"Lyddie's fine. I just walked to the road to get the mail and saw Ben..." she stopped and glanced at Carl, who hadn't lifted his head from his task. "...saw the sheriff. There's been a mine explosion. He needs help to rescue the miners. He asked if I could come to help make coffee and food."

"But the mine's closed. How can there be an explosion?" Will shook his head, confused.

"He said it was a bootleg mine near town."

Tom! Will sprang into action. "I need to let Sybil know where I'm going. You two meet me at the truck. I'll get some picks and shovels from the shed."

"You go, Will," Carl said. "I wouldn't be much good with this bad leg. I'll keep working here and check on Sybil and the baby later." His eyes moved to Eleanor. "I'll keep an eye on Danny too."

Will cast a grateful glance at Carl. "Thanks. It's good to know I can leave things in your hands." He rushed from the apple house, whispering a quick prayer. "God, let Tom be alive!" He drove the old truck at a high speed, thankful for the full tank of gas. He and Eleanor were there within the hour.

Nothing prepared them for the sight that greeted

them when they arrived. It looked as if an enormous monster had taken a bite out of the side of the mountain. The glaring hole had large rocks piled at the opening and still spewed out puffs of dirt into the air. A sizable crowd had already gathered. Some men dug through the rock and dirt as others hauled off large boulders in a human chain, passing them from one to the next until chunks of rock lay in a pile away from the work site.

Eleanor and Will spotted Benson's police car and headed toward it. Eleanor stopped and pointed to the ground where several sparrows lay lifeless. Will's throat constricted. "Methane gas," he whispered.

The sheriff met them and spoke in a low voice. "Will, Eleanor. Glad you're here."

"What do you know, Benson?" Will never took his eyes off the sparrows.

"Not much. As you can see, the likely cause is methane gas. No one knows how many were in the shaft. Since it's a bootleg operation, there's no records of how many miners are in there, or even what their names are."

"I know their names, Sheriff."

"Tom!" Will grabbed his friend's arm. "Thank God! I thought you were..."

Tom turned to the sheriff and admitted the truth. "I would have been, but something happened just as I arrived this morning. I left and didn't know about this until I was halfway home and heard the explosion."

He glanced back at Will. "Can I tell you about it later? I need to give names to the sheriff, then I'd like to get back to the digging." It was only then Will noticed

Tom's bloodied hands and the red-brown stains on his pants around his knees.

"Of course, I'll join the rest of the men."

"I'll go help with the coffee." Eleanor added.

"Eleanor, I think they have plenty of help," the sheriff said. "We need to set up a first aid station for the workers. Several of them already need medical help, starting with Tom. We're likely to have more rescue workers injured."

Benson motioned to a spot near his vehicle. "Over here, Tom. Eleanor can help those hands while you give me the names of the miners."

"Sheriff, I..." Tom said with a trembling voice.

"It's all right, Tom. We'll talk about the bootlegging later. Right now, we need to get these men out."

Will took a place in the human chain, heaving large rocks from the man on his left to the man on his right. He watched as more people arrived. Men silently picked up a shovel to dig or join the line to haul away the rocks. Others succumbed to tears when they saw the destruction. Soon a group of wives, some with babies in their arms and almost all with small children clinging to their dresses, formed a semi-circle around the workers. Pastor Gandy arrived and moved through the crowd to offer words of encouragement and an occasional prayer.

Each time Will glanced up from the line a small boy and a dog caught his attention. Occasionally, the boy would run over to a wagon where his mother sat with a passel of small children. Then he'd come back to the same spot, his dog faithfully following him back and forth. Will wondered if his father might be a miner trapped inside.

When his muscles screamed at him and his legs trembled from passing the large rocks, he walked over to get a cup of coffee and give his body a chance to recover. He took the coffee but refused a sandwich, though it was well past noon and he hadn't eaten since breakfast. His stomach constricted at the thought of food, too tight with tension to eat.

"Will! It's Tom, he's in there!" Emma screamed as she ran toward him.

He grabbed her arm to keep her from rushing to the mine opening. "Tom's okay. He wasn't in the mine when it exploded."

"No, you don't understand. It's his job. He's one of the miners." She struggled to get free of his hold.

"Emma, wait! I talked to him. He's helping with the rescue. He told me he came here to work this morning, but never went inside."

Understanding filled her eyes. "Oh, thank God. I was so frightened."

"The digging crew will change in a few minutes. They work in shifts. It's slow, exhausting work. You can talk to him then."

"The others? Are they alive?"

"We don't know yet. We haven't got to the mine's entrance yet. It's still a rescue mission, but..."

Shouting drew their attention to the crowd. "We're through! We're at the shaft entrance." Hope moved through the crowd like flowing water over rocks.

"Tom's going in." The shout came from Sheriff Eakins.

"Tom! Wait for me." Emma ran toward the opening, arriving just before Tom entered the narrow tunnel cleared by the crew. He gazed into his wife's eyes for a quick moment. "I love you, Emma. You and the boys." Then he disappeared into the mouth of the monster.

Silence settled once again over the crowd as they waited, hopeful Tom would return with a miner and news of the others. Emma and Will joined the vigil as seconds became minutes and minutes crawled into an hour.

Low whispers rippled through the crowd as fear and frustration rose. Will watched as the boy and his dog made a trip to the wagon. The children were asleep, sprawled out in the back of the wagon, legs and arms entangled. The mother followed her son back. They stood together, eyes glued to the shaft opening, silent tears streaming down both their faces.

Finally, a sound came from the tunnel. Will rushed forward with the other men, ready to help an injured miner. But only Tom crawled out, coughing and covered in dust. Emma rushed forward with a cup of water.

When he could talk, Tom whispered, "Will."

He leaned down close to where Tom lay on the ground.

"Tell the sheriff it's no longer a rescue mission. I've been to hell and back," Tom whispered before he passed out. Will didn't know if it was from exhaustion or the scene his friend had witnessed.

The boy remained at the site after his mother took his siblings home, hoping to see his father's body removed from the rubble. He grabbed snatches of sleep in the back of someone's truck and ate sandwiches provided by the women.

It took three more days to retrieve the bodies. The workers removed six miners, all of whom had lost their jobs at Berkley Coal Mine. The body of the young boy's father wasn't among them. When the workers stopped, unable to find the seventh miner, the boy refused offers to be driven home. He stayed planted at his place of vigil.

Will walked to where the boy stood and put one hand on his shoulder. "I'm sorry, son. Your father would be proud of the way you stayed until the end. It's time to go home now. Your mother will be needing you. Tell her we'll put a cross at the mine's entrance for your dad."

The boy finally started home, his dog trotting beside him.

Funerals began on the fourth day after the explosion. Exhausted, grim-faced family and friends came to pay their last respects. Many of them left one service and went straight to the next.

At the third funeral of the day, Will stood outside his small church, emotionally and physically spent. He gazed at the crowd, seeing many of the same faces he'd seen at the other services. Then he saw Tom walking toward him, leaning heavily on a cane. Crawling through the rubble inside the mine wrenched his back. He had a large bandage over his forehead where he'd slashed it open on a large bolder.

"Hello. Tom. How are you? I can say I've seen you looking better." Will smiled at his friend.

"Physically, I'm healing. Might take a little longer for my heart to get there."

Will nodded and remained silent, sensing Tom had joined him for a reason. He'd wait until his friend felt ready to tell him why.

"I've apologized to Emma. You're next."

He opened his mouth to protest when Tom held up his hand. "No, I need to get this out. I was rude to you in the diner that day. Reckon I'd been rude to everyone for a while. I don't have any excuse for my behavior, but God has forgiven me, and I'm here to ask you as well."

"It's okay, Tom. I forgave you before you even left the diner. Must be hard losing a job you'd worked at for years. I understand the stress to provide for a family."

"There's more. On the day of the explosion, I arrived at the mine at my designated time. We'd staggered our arrivals, so there was never a group of us outside the mine. We had to be careful about drawing attention to what we were doing. Even parked our vehicles in different places and walked to the mine. I got there last that day, so the other men were already working deep in the shaft."

He paused, then his voice became softer, more reflective. "The rest is harder to explain. Emma and I argued about the bootleg mine the night before the explosion. She wanted me to stop. I got angry and said things I never should have spoken."

Tom's voice broke, and he grew silent for a moment. "Her last statement stuck in my mind. She told me she'd rather have me with nothing than everything without me. When I got to the mine the next morning, what she said flew back to me. I reckon it winged its way into my stubborn heart and I couldn't go in. I knew then I was following my own path instead of seeking what God wanted in my life.

"I turned around and started back home to Emma. About half a mile from the mine, I heard the explosion. I rushed back." His eyes filled with tears. "I knew immediately methane caused the explosion. I've heard methane stories all my life, but never realized what it could do until I crawled into the shaft. The worst of it is, I'm the one who started the bootleg operation. All those men were my friends and I cost them their lives. I'll have to live with that now."

"Tom, I'm sorry you..."

"Don't feel sorry for me. My willfulness took the life of those men. I'm just thankful God got ahold of me that morning and made me see I needed to follow His way, not my own way."

He paused, then gave Will a sheepish grin. "Sheriff Eakins came by this morning and told me no charges would be filed against me because I'd risked my life to help after the explosion. So if you still need help with the harvest, I'd appreciate..."

"No need to ask, Tom. You're hired."

Movement at the church door pulled their attention. They watched as the wife of the deceased miner exited the church, surrounded by her three children, one of seven families left to make their way without a husband and father.

Chapter 30

A rising sun cast slanted rays of hopefulness across the fall sky. The sight strengthened Will's resolve to get the last of the apples harvested today. He stretched his sore muscles as he downed the last of his coffee. Time to meet Eleanor, Danny, and Carl at the apple house. Tom would be there soon. By his calculation, they'd finish with the picking by noon. Then came the tedious job of cleaning, sorting, and packing.

It had been a long month. The five of them had spent the last four weeks following the same schedule six days a week. After a rest on Sunday, Will loaded the week's harvest early each Monday morning to deliver them to his distributor. He stayed until his apples made it onto the train, trying not to be prideful of the way his apples shined compared to the others. Each time the train pulled out of the station he said a prayer of gratefulness.

This was the last of the harvest until late November, when the Red Delicious and Johnathan apples would be ready to pick. Now he'd have some time to practice his sign language and maybe even join Matilda on her visits with Tilly. He marveled at the way Matilda had embraced Tilly. An unlikely pair.

For years, Matilda bought joint medicine from Josiah, never knowing its source. The moment Will shared about meeting Tilly, she'd announced, "You must take me to meet her, Will." When he tried to protest, she interrupted.

"No, I want to meet this amazing woman who has brought me such relief from arthritis over the years. Something no doctor could do! If you won't take me, Will Parson, I'll tromp those woods until I find her."

Watching the two together at their first meeting amazed him. He knew immediately a fast friendship would form, a friendship destined to feed both of their souls.

He grabbed his cap when he saw his pickers pass the kitchen on their way to the apple house. Daisy met him when he stepped onto the porch, wagging her tail furiously. "Okay, girl. Let's get to work. You like these days in the orchard, don't you?" She gave a loud woof and raced ahead of him.

Danny and Eleanor loaded the wagon with empty apple baskets while Carl went to the barn to get Lucky. It surprised everyone when Carl took a liking to Will's old mule. Usually stubborn about being hitched to a wagon, the large animal seemed mesmerized by Carl's soft murmurings and gentle hands on the side of its neck. The mule followed him like a puppy. Without asking, Carl took over all of Lucky's care, seeing to his feed, water, and stall.

Will watched now as Carl walked to the open doors of the apple house, Lucky in tow. He'd learned to hitch him to the wagon after only one lesson.

"Morning, Carl. Looks like fit weather for our last day of picking."

Carl responded with a single nod. Will had become accustomed to this lack of communication. He appreciated the quiet steadiness Carl brought to his work. The man never complained, but seldom engaged in a male conversation Will craved.

"Mornin' all," Tom said as he entered the apple house. "Looks like a great day for picking. What do you say, Danny? Shall we take on Will and your father to see who picks the most?"

Danny giggled, "We win!"

Now here was a source of all the male talk he could ask for. It had been wonderful to have Tom's help with the harvest. He arrived early each morning with a smile and happy banter which Danny loved. Will knew Tom's happiness never reached the depths of his heart, which still grieved over the loss of the miners. Still, he was grateful for the fun Tom brought to the job of harvesting the apples.

With Tom's help, the baskets were in the wagon in short order, and the five of them headed to the orchard.

"Everyone, we'll be near the beehives today, so it would be wise to keep our voices low. I don't think they'll bother us, but they don't like loud noises." Will pointed to the hives at the edge of the woods and wondered if Tilly might be watching as they worked.

"I be quiet as mouse, Mr. Will." Danny laughed loudly at his own joke, then covered his mouth. "I sorry!"

"It's okay. Just talk in a normal voice, no yelling or loud laughs." This would be difficult for Danny, who liked to keep a lively chatter going.

"Okay," Danny mouthed with a thumbs up. Despite the warning, the adults broke into laughter.

"Let's just hope the bees like Danny's jokes as much as I do," Tom said.

Time to get this crew busy. "Tom, you, Eleanor, and Danny take these four rows, Carl and I will take the four closest to the beehives."

The next few hours moved along with the rhythm of work as each picker found the ripe apples. Tom was fast, faster even than Will as he scurried up and down the ladder picking the highest fruit, leaving the lower apples for Eleanor and Danny.

Will still shivered when he thought of the day Danny climbed the ladder and missed a rung in the middle coming down. He'd landed on the ground with a thud and a groan, which brought all of them to his side. He seemed fine after a careful examination, and his moans soon turned to belly laughs. "I fly, Mr. Will."

He wagged his finger at Danny. "No more flying, Danny. From now on you're grounded!" That brought even more belly laughs from the young man on the ground.

There were no other incidents except for a few blisters on feet and hands. His inexperienced pickers had risen to the challenge and Will thanked God for each of them.

The rumble of a motor car drew Will's attention to the road. Matilda waved as she passed the pickers on her way to help Sybil with the baby and get a meal ready for the pickers. Of all the blessings Will received during this harvest, she proved to be the greatest.

Without her daily appearance, usually bearing some delectable dessert, he'd no doubt Sybil would have folded a few days into the harvest, unable to bear the burden of childcare and meal preparation. Under Matilda's careful yet stern guidance, his wife was doing well with both. Will even thought her manner had softened, as he watched her with Lyddie in the evenings.

"Thank you, Matilda," he whispered from where he stood on his ladder.

The sun perched high overhead when they loaded the last basket heaped full of shiny apples onto the wagon. A sense of deep satisfaction and gratitude filled Will as he looked at the full wagon. He turned to his crew. "Well, that finishes this harvest for now. If you don't mind, I'd like to thank God for his goodness." He removed his cap, followed in suit by Carl, Tom, and Danny.

"Lord, thank you for your bountiful blessings of this season. Thank you for those who have worked to bring us to a full harvest. Bless them, Father, for all their hard labor. I'm grateful there have been no injuries in the past weeks, even though Danny tried to fly." A small ripple of laughter went through the group. "We are thankful for your provisions and benefits. In Jesus' name. Amen."

"Sybil, these are the best chicken and dumplings I've ever eaten. Thank you, sweetheart." Will smiled at his wife.

"And I'd like to thank whoever made this delicious cake," Tom mumbled through a mouthful of chocolate delight.

Sybil ducked her head to hide her blush. "The thanks should go to Matilda. It's her hen and her recipe. I just helped."

"Oh, go on with you all." Matilda waved her hand at them. "That old hen has been a thorn in my side for years. Most ornery chicken I've ever known. I had to boil her for hours just to get the stubbornness out of her. And the dumpling recipe came from Tilly. Seems she has other talents than making her wonderful medicines."

"Well, my praises to both the cooks and to Tilly," Eleanor said with a smile. "Now, let's get these dishes cleared up so we can sort and pack those apples."

"No, Eleanor, you go about the work in the apple house. Sybil and I will clean up in short order." Matilda's no-nonsense voice told the group she meant business. "As soon as we finish up here, I plan to have coffee with Tilly. I'll see you all back here tomorrow afternoon for Lyddie's birthday party. From the looks of how fast the cake is disappearing, I'll need to bake another one for tomorrow!"

"I'll be back with the family after church. We don't want to miss the baby's first birthday." Tom tweaked Lyddie's cheek, which she rewarded with a huge smile. "And I sure don't want to miss out on another chocolate cake!"

Will glanced at all that sat at his table, his heart as full as his belly.

A sudden strong wind sent a shower of multicolored leaves spiraling down from the oaks as Will stepped off the back stoop Sunday morning. A brilliant blue sky added to the beauty of the new day.

He surveyed the farmyard and saw Eleanor feeding the chickens, with Danny trailing behind her, determined to give each chicken a name.

"Morning, Eleanor, Danny. Feels like fall today, doesn't it?"

"It does. Makes my heart sing to be out in all this beauty." Eleanor smiled as she scattered grain on the ground.

"Danny, did you name all these ladies today?" Will teased.

"There's Retta." Danny pointed to a large red hen. "Can you make them be still, Mr. Will?"

"I'm afraid I can't help you with that. I'm no chicken whisperer."

Danny gazed at him for a moment, then lowered his voice to a whisper as he continued to point at each chicken. "Jenny, Flora, Missy..."

Will and Eleanor looked at each other with a grin.

"Carl about?"

"He's in the barn feeding Lucy. He's already fed the pigs."

"Is he going to join you at church this morning?"

"No, he says he needs to give the mule's stall a good mucking. Then he plans to bathe her. Says he wants Lucky to look good for the hayride." She smiled and shook her head slightly. "I think he's actually excited to drive the wagon. He's already filled it with hay."

Will waited, sensing Eleanor wanted to say more.

She studied the barn for a moment, then focused on Will, her eyes moist. "Carl would never say it, but I think he's happy here. He's not same man as the one who lived next door to you." A quick sob burst from her chest. "If you hadn't asked us to come here, I don't know what—"

"It wasn't me who brought you here. God did this, and I thank Him for the three of you every day. Now, I'd better get some hay out to the cows so I can get ready for church."

The sun cast a long shadow on the partygoers. By the time the hayride concluded, only a heap of crumbs remained of Matilda's cake. Lyddie lay in an exhausted sleep in Will's arms. In his mind, the party had been a great success. Even Sybil embraced the role of hostess and seemed pleased with all the compliments Lyddie received.

He sighed in disappointment over the fact that Tilly had refused to come. Will walked to her cabin three nights ago to invite her, shocked when she gave him a vehement "no." He tried again and watched as she pulled into herself. She refused to listen to another word about it.

He'd seen this behavior a few times before. It made him wonder even more about her past. His quiet, reclusive neighbor seemed like a bird with an injured wing who wanted to fly, but fear held her back. Who or what had broken her?

He rose from the rocker on the porch to take

Lyddie inside when he heard the roar of a car driving far too fast up the path to his house. Johnny Rhode jumped from the car almost before it came to a full stop. "I'm looking for my parents. Been searching for them for over a month. I'm willing to pay for any information about them." He glared at Will, his nose in the air, hands on his hips.

"You don't have to look any farther, son. We're right here."

Johnny spun around at the sound of Eleanor's voice. "Finally. Where have you been? I've hunted for you for weeks." He paused and glanced over his shoulder at Will, who watched the scene unfold. Then he turned back to his mother. "What do you mean, *you're here*? Where's *here*?"

"In the foreman's cottage." Eleanor pointed over her shoulder.

"Why? And where's Dad?" Johnny's voice rose and became more urgent.

"He's unhitching the wagon and putting the mule in his stall," she said with a smile. "He took us on a hayride for the baby's birthday celebration."

Will watched her face. Was she was enjoying telling her son about their employment? He knew he was! Then he chastised himself as the second commandment came to mind, *love your neighbor as yourself.*

Eleanor spoke again. "Why don't you come to the cottage? We'll talk over a cup of coffee." She stepped closer to Johnny and placed a gentle hand on his back. "I'm sure this father wants to get his sleeping baby out of the night air."

Will watched as they walked away, then turned to

go inside. What he saw next stopped him in his track. Sybil stood in the window with an expression on her face that caused the old fear to once again surface.

Chapter 31

Cold air and heavy dark clouds threatened a snowstorm before evening. Will pulled his cap closer to his ears and wished he'd grabbed his wool knit cap before leaving the house this morning.

He jammed the claw hammer behind the plank on the side of the barn, then ripped it away from the studs. It pulled loose with little resistance, and he moved to the plank below, estimating he'd have all the rotten wood finished by noon.

"Will, I need your help!" Eleanor shouted from the bottom of the ladder.

"I can't right now. I need to finish this job before the snow comes," he said as he tugged on the hammer. "Ask Johnny or Carl to help with whatever you need— and move back, please. I'm about to drop another piece of wood."

"I can't do that." She raised her voice while stepping back from the wood stack. "Johnny left this morning and Carl's cold is worse. Please come down. There's something important I need to tell you."

Curious, he made his way down the ladder. "What is it? If I don't get this barn repaired before the snow comes, Lucky will spend a chilly night in there tonight." He jerked his thumb over his shoulder.

Eleanor paused, then sighed. "Sybil and Johnny left early this morning." She looked at the toes of her shoes, then back at Will. "I would've come to tell you as soon as she left, but Carl was too sick. He's resting now. It's the first time I felt safe to leave him."

"Sybil left with Johnny? I don't understand. Did she need to go to town? Why didn't she..." He reached out to steady himself on the ladder as a memory of the early morning came back and a dreaded thought made its way to his brain.

"She's left us, hasn't she?" his voice was barely above a whisper. "She woke early this morning to write a letter." He stared at the house and continued, "I thought it might be to her parents. The letter is for me, isn't it?" He turned questioning eyes to Eleanor.

"Yes, she told me she left a letter for you on..."

"Lyddie Anne!" He started for the house.

She grabbed his arm to stop him. "The baby's fine. Danny's watching her at the cottage. I tried to call the doctor on your telephone, but it's dead. I hate to ask you to go for the doctor, but Carl is very ill. I'm afraid it's pneumonia. Can you do this for me, please?"

He shook his head, trying to focus on what she'd said, but her words came as if in a tunnel.

"Will, are you listening? We need a doctor!"

"Yes, of course I'll go. Let me get some things from the house."

He raced through the kitchen door and up the stairs. He'd mailed the money for the telephone bill a week ago. If it had been lost in the mail, or stolen, he'd have to get more money from the emergency fund. Did he have enough to pay the bill for a second time? Will stopped when he saw the letter propped on his pillow as reality set in. He stared at it for a moment, then stuffed it in his coat pocket with such a force, it crumbled in his fist.

The twenty-mile trip to Berkley did little to soothe his anger. Hot fury swelled within him, most of it directed at Sybil. How could she leave their daughter?

He stopped at Dr. Jennings's office to request he go to Carl, then headed to the telephone company.

"Henry," Will said with a nod as he walked into the small office just off the square.

"Will, you're here. Uh..." Henry looked down at his desk and back at Will's face.

"I won't say that's the smartest thing you've ever said, Henry. But, yes, I'm here."

"Well, um, what can I do for you?"

"I'm sure you know. I'm here to pay my phone bill." He dug in his pants for the money. "How much is the late fee? I need my phone back on as soon as possible. We have a sick worker at the farm."

"You did pay your bill. I got the payment two days ago in the mail. But Sybil came by when I first opened this morning. She said you decided to get rid of the phone. Asked if you could have the payment back. It's only been off for a few hours. I'll waive the late fee." Henry glanced past him to look out at his parked truck, then lowered his voice. "Will, she was with Johnny Rhode."

His jaw tightened as he placed the money on the counter and left without a word.

Will drove the twenty miles back home haphazardly, determined to think of nothing but Lyddie. He imagined for the hundredth time the look on his daughter's face when she saw her first lit Christmas tree in just a few days.

A new thought surged through his mind. "That's it! It's Christmas," he said in a loud voice. "Sybil wants to surprise us with gifts. That's why she talked Henry into returning the money from the phone bill. She probably asked Johnny to drive her to Lewisburg." He let out a small laugh. "She'll be home by dinner."

Then he remembered the letter. He pulled off to the side of the road, where the trees made a beautiful backdrop for the valley below. In the distance, Old Bald Mountain lay in a shroud of haze, snow already collected at the higher altitude. He pulled the crumpled letter from his pocket and smoothed it on his thigh.

Dear Will,

I'm sorry. I want you to know I tried to be a good wife to you and a mother to Lyddie Anne but it's too hard. I'm not meant to be a farmer's wife. It's just too bad I didn't realize it before we got married.

You must believe I love Lyddie—her soft curly hair and her sweet smile will always be in my memories. But I can't take care of a deaf child. It's better for her if I'm not around.

Forgive me for taking the telephone money.
Fondly, Sybil

He tore the letter into shreds and let the small pieces fly down the valley as the snow started to fall on his shoulders.

Eleanor and Will helped Dr. Jennings lift Carl to listen to his lungs, although it seemed a moot point. Wheezing echoed through the cottage. The familiar chuffing filled Eleanor with dread. Her Grandfather Kinser's breathing sounded the same the night he passed. She wanted to escape the agony of it.

The doctor motioned for them to follow him out of the bedroom.

"Why did you wait so long to get me, Eleanor? Both of Carl's lungs have fluid in them," the doctor said, frustration obvious in his voice.

"He didn't want a doctor. He said it was just a head cold. I've tried to get him to come see you for two weeks now."

"Two weeks! No wonder he's so sick. It's more than a head cold now." He lowered his voice and continued. "He could go either way. Keep him propped up with pillows and get some steam in the room with pots of boiling water. It may help the breathing. I have another house call to make but I'll be back around sunset."

Eleanor swayed, and Will and Dr. Jennings helped her to the sofa. "Sit a minute, Eleanor. Will, make her some strong coffee? It'll be a long day."

"Sure, Doc. I'll do what I can."

After the doctor left, Eleanor drank a few swallows of the coffee, then turned to Will. "I need two pots of boiling water. Can you bring them into the bedroom before you leave?" She paused, deliberating what to say next. "I know you're hurt by Sybil's leaving. But please try to have kind thoughts about her. She may decide to return. I'm so sorry my Johnny had a part in this."

"You don't have anything to apologize for. This is the doing of those two together. Truth be, it probably would have happened sooner or..."

"Please don't be bitter." Eleanor interrupted. "Lyddie will miss her mother. I'll help all I can, you know that. But your daughter needs you even more now." She sighed. Her shoulders ached, her bones already tired. "Why don't you take her to your place now? And take Danny, please. I think it's best if he weren't in the cottage today." She didn't wait for any answer, simply walked back into the bedroom to attend to the task ahead of her.

"Eleanor." Carl's raspy voice was low.

She felt a great dread rising within her. "Shh. Don't talk, Carl. Just rest."

"No. Must say this." A spasm of coughing spewed from his throat, so strong the bed shook. Eleanor gave him a sip of water.

When he continued speaking she leaned over to put her ear close to his mouth. "There's a box in the attic behind the old wardrobe. Get the letter. Tell her I'm sorry."

"Carl, you don't know what you're saying. It's the fever, dear. Please rest."

"It's important. Promise—" The cough returned with a vengeance this time. After several minutes, he tried again. "Promise me!"

"All right. I promise." Fear and a deep grief for all they'd missed in their marriage threatened to overtake her emotions. A sob escaped her throat.

"Eleanor. Please forgive—" A shortness of breath interrupted his words. "I love you and Danny." Another rack of coughs left him exhausted, and he sank deeper into the bedding.

The sun had set when Dr. Jennings returned. He found Eleanor sitting in her rocker in the dark front room, no lanterns lit, no water boiling.

"Eleanor?"

"He passed an hour ago. Just went quietly," she said. "Something to be thankful for, I suppose, a peaceful death."

They buried Carl two days later. Services were held in the Lick Creek Bible Church. Eleanor, Danny, Will, Benson, Matilda and the Spriggs were the only ones who attended. They sat huddled close to the front of the church, where the pot-bellied stove offered some warmth.

Pastor Gandy delivered the message. "Carl Rhode lived much of his life with a greed and a hardness which created unhappiness for many around him. But I believe none suffered more than he himself did. Scripture says if we confess our sins, God is faithful and just to forgive and purify. Carl and I had a few conversations before his death in which he made known his great regret for his actions. He asked God to forgive him. Let us honor him now for the great courage this act took and have mercy on his soul."

Eleanor sat stone still. *Carl went to see Pastor Gandy? Why didn't he tell me? I should have let him be more open with me—trusted him more.* Grief for all the time they'd lost welled up in her. Tears she'd held at bay for the last three days flowed down her cheeks with abandon.

Well past midnight on the day of the funeral, she lay awake, her soul tormented. She should have tried to communicate more—to let Carl know her pride in his work on the farm. Years of resentment kept her from it.

The letter! She'd not thought of it since the last conversation with her husband. *I must see if it's there. I need to trust him now.*

Chapter 32

*T*illy smiled when she saw Matilda lumbering
through meadow, headed to her cabin. Somehow,
she knew her friend would come today. She'd told
Matilda on their last visit that she'd be grinding willow
bark to make for a healing tea for the flu on Monday.
And here she came, eager to learn more from Tilly's
wealth of knowledge.

"I'll say this for her, Solomon. She's got a hunger
for learnin' like I've ain't never seen. Don't reckon
there's anything she don't want to know."

She turned and put the kettle on to boil and
reached for a plate of cold biscuits left from breakfast.
"Come on in, Matilda. Got coffee and breakfast
biscuits." Tilly smiled as she spoke, amazed by her
own friendliness. But then, a body would have to be
half dead not to welcome the likes of Matilda.

Since their first meeting, Matilda had come
to the cabin at least once a week. She never came

empty-handed, and Tilly made sure her new friend never left empty-handed. Her shelves were filled now with a large variety of jellies and jams. A box of brand-new candles and a tin of lamp oil sat unopened on the table.

Best of all were the books. Matilda introduced Tilly to Faulkner's *As I Lay Dying,* where she read about the Bundren family's trek through Mississippi on a pilgrimage to bury their wife and mother. And to the Nancy Drew mysteries. She stayed awake reading *The Secret of the Old Clock* until the early hours of the morning, eager to find out who done it.

Their conversation over coffee often turned to the Bible. Tilly absorbed the Word, but she still had many questions. Today she asked a difficult one. "Matilda, does God deliver everyone from trouble?"

"I swear, Tilly, you ask tough questions. Twice now I've gone to see Pastor Bill to get help." She shrugged her shoulders and continued, "Yes, I think he must if you ask him to."

"Well, I don't think he does—not every time. At least not for me." Tilly picked up the coffee mugs and put them in the sink. She grabbed a cloth and scrubbed the counter, as if she could wipe away her frustration.

Matilda spoke in a soft, kind voice. "You know, Tilly, if you tell me the cause of the sadness always present in your eyes, you might discover the answer to your question."

Tilly considered the request for several moments. Maybe the time to share her story had come. She moved to her rocker and began a slow, determined back-and-forth motion. Her eyes looked down at the braided rug under her feet as memories moved from hazy to distinct with each rock.

"Happened a long time ago when I was thirteen." She spoke in a monotone voice to hide the surge of emotions flooding her veins. "I shoulda knowed better, but he said there was baby kittens in the shed—said I could have my pick. I never got to pick the best of anything. Big Mama said it was a sin to covet." She stopped, her thoughts filled with her grandmother.

Matilda waited without a word.

"He acted nice until he closed the door. Then he got mean. Push me to the dirt floor and held me down. He raised my dress and pushed himself into me. I tried to get away, but he was too strong."

Tilly stopped, silent for many moments before she continued. "My arm got loose, and I reach out for a crowbar I'd seen on the ground when I went in. Hit him on the back of his leg, hard. Hard 'nough to hear a crack. When he let go, I scrambled up and run outa the shed."

More silence. "I hurt him bad. I ran back to Big Mama and cried in her arms. She packed up some things and brung me here right way. Told me to live like a man and to never come out of the woods. Said I'd go to prison or worse if I did."

She looked up at Matilda then, tears streaming down her cheeks. "I been here all these years. I don't think God delivered me that day."

"Oh, my dear friend." Matilda whispered, her own face wet. She reached for Tilly's hands and said, "I think he's delivering you now."

Later in the afternoon, Tilly walked to the river with lead feet and a shroud of remembrance heavy about her. She'd broken her promise to Big Mama and told her story. Her grandmother's voice played in her head the rest of the day. *Don't let nobody find you, and never tell what happened.* She'd done both. Even made friends.

Now she wanted to hide in her cabin until the claws of fear loosened. But she needed to meet Josiah. She had a delivery for him, and he had staples for her.

She arrived at the river's edge and saw the skiff cutting through the deep, still waters headed to the wide bend in the river, which provided a perfect place for the boat to come to the bank. As the craft got closer, panic rose in her chest. It held three persons.

Pain grabbed her, tightening like a vise. So tight, she clutched her arm across her chest. Should she run? The pain lessened as she backed into the low branches of a spruce, where she could see but not be seen.

A man, boy really, paddled the boat to the edge of the bank and tied it off. Josiah stood and called out, "Now, Tilly. I know yous hidin'. Come on out. No need to be afeared of my family. I needed help today. Gots the ache in my joints. Cain't handle the oars. This ain't nobody 'cept my oldest son, Trey, and my wife."

He chuckled. "Sadie Mae wouldn't hear o' me bringin' nobody else 'less she come too. Reckon she wants to know who I been meetin' up with all these years. Good lookin' man like me." His chuckle went into a full belly laugh, rocking the small skiff.

"Josiah Smith, stop your talk and get outa this boat afore you dump all three of us in the river!" Sadie said. "Tilly, I'd sure like to meet you. Knew your grandma well. Come on out, now. We bring you no harm."

She knew Big Mama. The pull was too strong, and Tilly moved beyond the low branch toward them. By then, all three were out of the boat and her staples lay in a box on the smooth grass.

Sadie took a step toward Tilly. "My, you do look like Masie Sayre. Masie started comin' to River Town AME Church years ago. Had the most beautiful voice God ever give a body. The church filled with joy when Masie sang." She tilted her head and gave Tilly's face a long stare. "But I never saw the joy in her eyes. Always a sadness about her. Didn't know why, but now I do. She told me once 'bout a granddaughter she done sent to live with her brother in Chicago. Said you'd fare better there. She missed ya a powerful lot. Her eyes always told me that."

Tilly nodded, her voice too choked for words. She missed Big Mama too, though anger at the position thrust on her so many years ago surfaced often now. *Why, Big Mama? Why didn't you send me to Chicago? I could've had a life there, not these years all alone.* She finally croaked out a greeting. "Nice to meet ya."

She laid an eye on Trey and said with a nod, "You, too." He'd been ogling her since she walked up, no doubt shocked by a woman dressed in men's clothing.

"Afternoon," he said with the squeaky voice of an adolescent boy.

"Here's what groceries I could get," Josiah said as he wobbled his way to her. "Coffee's scarce these days, but I managed to get one bag. Most o' the rest on your list be there, too. I hope you got my joint ointment, and some for Miz Stotler. She been fussing for me to get down here and bring 'er some."

"It's here," Tilly said. Matilda could have gotten her potions directly, but had promised to keep their visits a secret. It comforted Tilly to know Matilda kept her word.

"We best be going. Gets dark early this time o' year."

"Tilly, I want to come back with Josiah one day so we can have a friendly visit," Sadie Mae said. "Will you let me come?"

She hesitated a moment, Big Mama's warning once again in her thoughts. *Enough, Big Mama. I need this.* "Yes."

She took her staples back to the cabin, then spent the rest of the day in the woods, relieved that the snow from the recent storm had melted enough to let her do some foraging. Just before dark, as she started home, the sudden sound of a small branch cracking caused her to crouch low. Footsteps, more than one set, came her way at a fast sped.

This time her chest didn't just hurt, it exploded. The jolt of pain sent her to her knees. She had to get undercover, but fear and pain paralyzed her body. *Who is that? Why they be running?* Unable to stand, she crawled under some cedar bushes, then made her way to a low spruce as two young black men stopped just beyond her.

"Do you even remember where you tied the boat?"

"Course I do," the tall one spat out a reply. "You think I'm stupid or somethin'?"

"Stupid enough not to wear a mask into that store."

"I tol' you, I couldn't breathe."

"Well, breath now so we can get goin'. Been here too long a'ready."

"Not till you get rid of that gun. I ain't gonna go down river in the dark with that thing. You know what'll happen if some white feller stops us and finds it!" He leaned against a wide oak, his feet planted.

"You know what this gun cost? If you wasn't my brother, I'd drop you where you stand." He took the gun from his pants and pointed it at the boy leaning on the tree with a jeer, then tossed it into the cedar bushes. "Happy? Now get a move on!"

Tilly stayed under the spruce until well after dark, afraid the boys might not have found the boat and were still wondering around the forest. She moved in her zig-zag pattern, going far away from the cabin. Finally satisfied, she walked back home. Her breaths came in quick puffs, and she longed for her bed.

She spent the rest of the night thrashing about, thinking of the events of the day. Sharing her story, meeting Josiah's family, and hiding from the two young boys threw her off base. She needed to find her center again.

Just before daylight, she heard a soft whisper in her heart. *Trust me, Daughter. I'm delivering you.*

Chapter 33

*F*rosted air blew from Will's mouth as he scrambled up the rise on the land near his home. He wanted to get to the clearing before the sun rose. Heavy fog lay over the mountains, and he hoped it would lift early. He needed to make a kill and get back to take care of Lyddie.

The past three months with Sybil gone had been difficult and lonely. Eleanor proved a godsend, helping care for Lyddie while he attended to the farm chores. Will's resentment and anger sat on his shoulders like a heavy winter coat while Eleanor struggled with her own grief. To make it worse, teething made his fifteen-month-old daughter cranky. Even Danny lost some of his cheerfulness as he tried to understand the death of his father.

The two families had Christmas at Matilda's home—a welcome respite from the burdens they felt. On Christmas afternoon, he and his hostess had a private conversation while Eleanor put Lyddie down for a nap.

"You've let bitterness make you hard and withdrawn, Will. Part of Lyddie's behavior results from the coldness you've wrapped around your heart. You don't just miss your wife; you're vehemently angry with her. Try to find some peace." Matilda stopped to see if her words hit the mark. "She may come home, and if she does, she'll need a softer heart than you have right now."

Will watched the fire as he drank a swallow of the hot apple cider Matilda served her guests after a bountiful Christmas meal. "I've said before, she made her choice. Reckon we just need to get on with life and accept it." But he couldn't move on. Even at the worst of times when Sybil made his life miserable, he loved her. The loss cut through him like a knife.

"Time to gather everyone," he said as he stood and put his cup down. "It'll be dark by time we get home and I've animals to feed."

The next morning behind a shelter of trees, he stared into a clearing and remembered the conversation with Matilda. Could he soften his heart if Sybil returned, when it felt colder than the wind blowing off the mountains?

The fog lifted as the warmth of the early morning sun cast its rays. At the edge of the clearing stood a magnificent eight-point buck, large enough to provide much needed meat for the three of them. Will took aim but couldn't pull the trigger. The beauty and freedom of the noble animal stunned him. He couldn't take the buck from this earth. Turning, he retraced his steps down the rise.

Halfway home, he spotted a young yearling doe. He made a clean shot and gutted it in quick time. As he worked, his thoughts went to Lyddie and her needs. With Sybil gone, he'd little time to practice his sign language now. Maybe he should think of the deaf school again.

Closer to home, Will found two rabbits in his traps. With ample meat for a good while, he no longer felt guilty about not killing the larger deer. He didn't have it in him to kill the buck—not today. With the rabbits shoved into the pockets of his hunting jacket, he carried the rifle in one hand and used the other to drag the small deer behind him.

On his trek home, Will decided to visit with Emma soon. He needed to know all he could about the school for the deaf. He'd take her and the boys some of the venison, since Tom had left just after the first of the year to work at a WPA dam project in Kentucky.

It surprised him to see Matilda's car at his house. He left the meat in the cellar before entering. Matilda sat in the kitchen having a cup of coffee with Eleanor.

"Morning, Matilda. You're here mighty early."

"I've good reason to be here early. We've got a genuine crisis and I need both your help. I've just been sharing it with Eleanor over a quick cup. But I've not got much time."

"Tell me what's going on. I'll do what I can to help."

"I hope so. We've got to convince Tilly to come to the sheriff's office in Berkley. They arrested Josiah Smith's son and his friend, Joe, for armed robbery. As usual, they've wasted no time on cases like this to get them to trial. It starts first thing in the morning in

Lewisburg. I fear this will not turn out well if we don't intervene."

"I don't understand. What does Tilly have to do with this?"

Eleanor spoke up. "Josiah went to Matilda's last night. He told her Trey went with him to see Tilly yesterday when the robbery happened. There's no way his son could have committed the crime. Tilly needs to tell the sheriff."

"The problem is getting her to agree to leave the woods." Matilda stood up with a grunt. "Well, I intend to get her there, even if I have to hog-tie and pull her. We can't let this go to trial. Not when so many like this end up in a hanging. I'd appreciate it if you two would go with me to the cabin."

Will flew into action. "Eleanor, you go with Matilda to the cabin. The two of you are more likely to convince her to go than me. I'll take Lyddie and Danny to Emma at the diner. I'll meet you on the steps of the sheriff's office."

He started up the stairs to get his daughter, then turned back to the two women. "Matilda, try not to kill Tilly with your driving before you get to the courthouse. She may have never ridden in a car, and Lord bless her if she's riding with you."

"I'll get her there safe enough, Will Parson. You just make sure you're on those steps of the jailhouse when we get there."

Dread draped itself over Tilly when Matilda and Eleanor appeared together. Did this bring another change? How much more would crash in on her? Then her heart heard soft-whispered words, "I'm delivering you."

Taking a deep breath, she moved toward them in the meadow. "Morning, Miz Matilda, Miz Eleanor. Everything okay?"

"We hope it will be soon. We need your help. Josiah Smith's son is about to go on trial for armed robbery. Josiah said he was here with you yesterday when it happened. He needs you to come tell the sheriff Trey came here with his father." Matilda held her hand up before Tilly could respond. "Now, before you say no, you need to trust me. What we talked about yesterday won't be a problem."

"We'll both be at your side every step of the way," Eleanor whispered.

Tilly's chest seized and pulled at every muscle around her ribcage. She struggled to stay on her feet. *Don't go out of these woods, Tilly. You're not safe.* Big Mama's words again. But in the next moment, she knew the time had come. She could never say no to Josiah's request for help.

Without another word, she turned and walked back to the cabin. She opened her trunk and shook out the white blouse and a denim skirt. After three and a half decades, Tilly Sayre left the woods.

True to his word, Will stood on the steps of the sheriff's office when Matilda's car made a screeching stop, tipping her two passengers forward in their seats. The party of four entered the station without a word.

Will stepped up to the deputy's desk. "Sheriff here?" he asked.

"Yeah. He's in his office," the young, lean officer

said as he gawked at the unlikely assembly before him. "I'll see if he's available."

"No need," Will said briskly. "He'll want to hear what we say. I know the way." He led the ladies to a back office.

A hard rap on the door brought a sharp response from the sheriff. "Jack, I told you not to disturb me. I'm buried in paperwork!"

"It's me, Benson. I've got Eleanor and two others with me." Will stuck his head inside the office.

The entire conversation took less than thirty minutes. Tilly told her story quietly, staring straight into the eyes of the sheriff. Benson asked a few questions before he dispatched a deputy and his other officer to locate the gun in the woods. Will went with the officers to help them navigate the woods.

Tilly sat on a bench outside the sheriff's office with Matilda and Eleanor on each side. Her hands, a sweaty mess while she'd spoken to the sheriff, had gone icy cold. She pressed them deep into the folds of her skirt.

None of them spoke. They glanced at each other when they heard a crowd gathering outside. News had traveled fast. Friends of the Smiths soon assembled on the steps and lawn. They'd heard about Tilly coming to town and the news she brought with her. At the front of the crowd stood Josiah and Sadie Mae.

Two hours later, the officers returned with the bagged gun. Benson conferred with them in his office, then stepped into the hallway and spoke to Tilly. "Miss Sayre, the gun has been found. If the fingerprints on the weapon prove to be someone other than Trey's or

Joe's, the boys will be released. You can go home now. Thank you for your help today."

Tilly waited, unable to speak. Surely he would arrest her now. He had to know about the crime committed so many years ago. She sat with her head down, even though Eleanor and Matilda were on their feet.

"Tilly," Eleanor whispered. "It's over. We can head back now."

"I told you everything would be okay." Matilda spoke next. "Let us take you back to your cabin." She paused, then continued. "I'm real proud to call you my friend, Tilly Sayre. It took courage to do what you did today."

She stood then. The thought of being back home gave strength to her legs.

On the sidewalk, on the grass, people waited. When Tilly emerged from the front doors, a spontaneous clap broke out. She shielded her eyes from the sun with her hand and stared over the crowd, her heart running a race in her chest. *Surely not for me?*

As she walked through the crowd, first one, then another, shook her hand.

"Miss Tilly, I knew your grandmother. A fine woman."

"I hope you'll join us at the River Town AME Church soon. Masie was much loved there."

"That took guts, Tilly. We're proud of you."

She nodded and smiled as they moved through the crowd. For the first time in many years, the heavy cloak she had worn for so long lifted.

Chapter 34

*E*leanor wheezed as she shook the dusty rug, then placed it on the line to give it a good beating. Spring had arrived. She needed to clean both the cottage and Will's house. It had been three months since Carl's death, and she still woke each morning filled with a loss she never thought would be there. Her grief left her drained most days.

Now she had to think of future—hers and Danny's. She couldn't stay on at Applewood Orchard forever, even if she spent most of her day helping Will with Lyddie and some of the farm chores. He needed a foreman, not a widow and her son.

She finished beating the first rug from the cottage and moved on to the second when she saw the sheriff's car roll to a stop out front. She pushed a piece of loose hair under the scarf tied to her head and wiped her dusty hands on her apron, then walked to the car.

"Hello, Benson. Picked a nice day for a drive."

"Sure did, one of the nicest. In fact, I thought you might like to take a ride with me."

"A ride? Well, I'm busy right..."

"It won't take long, I promise. There's something I want to show you."

The look in his eyes made her release the scarf, take off her apron, and call out to Danny.

"Danny, I'm going for a ride with the sheriff. You go on up to Will's house and see if Lyddie is awake. I'm sure he can use some help.

"Okay, Mama. I go help."

"You're the best helper, Danny."

"I know, Mama." Danny said with his big smile. He waved at Benson and shouted, "Bye. See you later, alligator!"

"Well, Benson. Let's go see what this mystery is all about," Eleanor said as she laid her apron in the back seat of the sheriff's car. "Am I helping you solve a case?"

"No, just out for a ride with a friend," Benson said with a smile.

Sitting beside him in the sheriff's car brought back a memory of the day they waited in the older version of the same vehicle. The day Carl always thought... *No, I won't think of that. Not on this beautiful day.*

Benson pulled onto the road and turned right. They drove past the apple orchard, a white blur from the spring's blooms. She smiled, thinking how it looked like low-lying white clouds. In short order, they slowed and turned into the Rhode estate.

"Why are we coming here?" She looked at him, confused. "What could you possibly want to show me at the estate?"

"Look at the foreclosure sign, Eleanor, please."

She glanced over his shoulder to see the word *Sold* painted over the sign. "Do you know who bought it? I can't imagine it selling in these hard times."

"I bought it, Ellie." He used her given name, then offered her a smile as big as a crescent moon. "I've saved for years and I had a little money from the passing of an uncle. I always wanted to raise beef cows. This is the perfect place for it."

"Oh, Benson. I'm so happy for you."

"Be happy for both of us, Ellie. I bought it for you and Danny and me." He continued before she could protest. "Hear me out, please. I know it's soon after Carl's death. But I can wait. I've already waited a lifetime for you. I'm retiring at the end of this year. I want to chase cows, not crooks," he said with a small smile, then became serious. "I'll give you and Danny all the time you need. Just tell me you'll think about it. I need to know that much."

She looked into the eyes of the man who had been so kind to her—a steady rock in her life. It felt right. "Yes, I'll think about it. I promise."

"Wonderful. Let's get out and walk. I'd like to share my plans for the place. I plan to tear the staircase down and replace it with a smaller one closer to one wall. Never did like a staircase that twisted."

Her heart swelled. Was there nothing this man wouldn't do for her? Then she remembered. The box in the attic! How could she have forgotten? She stopped and turned to Benson. "Do you have a key? Can you get in?"

"Sure do, just haven't used it yet. I wanted to

talk to you first. But are you sure you want to go in? It might be hard," he said, concern in his eyes.

"It's all right. I'd like to. There's something personal in the attic which I hope is still there."

The padlock released with slight pressure, and the big door opened. Bits of dust bunnies filled the bright morning sunlight. She paused in the foyer as memories flooded her. *No, I won't let that happen. This is Benson's home now and I'll honor that.* She moved up the staircase to the attic with quiet determination.

The attic door was harder to open, swollen by the recent spring rain. Once inside, Eleanor let her eyes adjust to the low light, then looked around. The attic had stacks of old furniture, chests, and outgrown toys. Three boxes of Christmas decorations were stuffed to overflowing. A thin layer of dust lay over everything, as if a light snow had just fallen. She spotted the wardrobe on the opposite wall and made her way through the rubble, then turned to Benson.

"Help me pull this away from the wall, please."

He paused only a second, then grabbed the piece of furniture with his massive arms and pulled it from the wall single handedly. There in the wall was a hole where the wall boards were removed. And in the hole sat a small wooden box.

Eleanor stepped up and pulled the box out, then went to stand by the light from the window. "This must be it. It's what Carl told me about right before he died."

Benson stared at the box, then at her, but didn't respond. She pulled a small stool from nearby and sat down, perching the box on her knees. Opening it, she found an envelope and a formal document. She opened the letter first and read it aloud.

To Whom It May Concern,

Bound in this box is a deed of trust for eighteen acres of land to the west of this estate. I have signed this deed over to Tilly Sayre for the act thrust upon her by my errant 15-year-old son. He not only hurt the girl but he sustained an injury on his left leg during the assault on her. I passed it off as a football injury from the private school I sent him to after the incident.

I'm not proud of my part in this tragedy, but he's my son, and I had to protect him until he became a man. God forgive me if what I did was wrong.

I can't apologize while in this life— that's for my son to do. It's his choice. He knows about this deed of trust and of my wishes for him to find the time and place to make things right. I'm hopeful when he's a grown man, he'll see the need to set things straight. Until then, I can only pray God will protect Miss Sayre and help her to not have hatred in her heart over what my son did to her.

Carl Rhode, Senior

She laid the letter back into the box and unfolded the deed and handed it to Benson.

He glanced over it and quietly said, "It looks official, but it'll need to go to a lawyer."

"Oh, Benson. No wonder Carl had such a tormented soul. How awful for the both of them. So young and so much stolen from them." Her eyes filled with tears for the two wasted lives.

Chapter 35

"**N**o, Lyddie. Danger!" Will signed the word by pulling his knuckles over the back of his fist while shaking his head and giving her a big frown. He bent down to make sure she could see him. He waited a second to see if she would move away from the garden hoe, proud when she did. Having Lyddie in the garden brought Will so much pleasure, but he had to watch her like a hawk to keep her safe.

He knelt before her and signed, "Time for lunch."

Lyddie reached for his hand, rewarded him with a big smile, and signed the word for hungry. His heart melted each time she communicated with him, and he wished again for more time to practice his signing. Still, they had a decent vocabulary, and she'd recently been using her words more often.

Will never spoke to Emma about the state school. His heart squeezed with pain at the thought of sending her away. No, as long as she was safe and happy, he'd keep her here. He couldn't stand to lose another family member. Just as he thought, he'd not heard a word from Sybil. Will assumed by now she'd made her way far from West Virginia, as she followed Johnny Rhode's latest scheme.

"Will, Will!"

He glanced up to see Eleanor rushing toward the garden.

"It's Tilly. She's sick. Matilda and I went there for coffee this morning and found her lying in the yard. I called for Doctor Jennings, but we need help to get her into her bed." She stopped and put her hand on her hip and bended from the waist. Her breathing came deep and fast. "I'll keep Lyddie. You go on."

Will flew into action as he swept up Lyddie and placed her into Eleanor's arms. "I'll take the truck close as I can to the path's opening in case we need to get her to a hospital, then walk on in." He planted a quick kiss on Lyddie's head and raced toward his truck.

When he reached the cabin, he found Tilly on the ground, awake but breathing hard.

Matilda stood up from where she was sitting beside her and took a few steps toward Will. "Wait, we must be careful of what we say. She's in a lot of pain but seems to understand me. I don't know how long she's been like this—she's stone cold. I covered her up as best I could. Now we need to get her inside and bank up the fire."

Will nodded and moved to where she lay on the grass. "Miss Tilly, I'm sorry you're feeling poorly. I need to lift you now to get you inside. Don't be afraid."

He held his breath, relieved when she didn't resist his touch.

Inside, Matilda changed her into dry night clothes while Will went to fetch firewood. His hands shook as he gathered wood sticks and kindling. The sound of her breathing and the bluish color of her lips frightened him. He'd seen this before and knew her heart was failing.

Heart! Maybe she had some medicine for an ailing heart.

He raced back inside, nearly dropping the load of firewood. "Matilda, ask her what medicine we should give her. She must have something her for the heart."

"Tilly, dear." Matilda leaned close. "We need your help. What medicine do we need to give you?"

"Hm... hm."

Matilda looked at Will in panic. "I don't think she can tell us."

"Then I'll bring all the bottles to her," he said as he headed for the door. "Maybe she can show us."

He flew to the shed and gathered one of every powder he could find.

Back inside, he methodically showed Tilly the medicines, until she finally reached out and touched the ground dandelion root.

"Matilda, I think this is it. Should we make some tea? The bottle says fluid."

"I'll put a pot on to boil," she said as she moved toward the sink.

Then Will noticed Tilly patting on her chest. He retraced his steps, and she pointed to the rest of the medicine bottles. "You want another one?" She shook her head yes, and he began the process again, showing her one bottle at a time." When he held up the hawthorn berries, she closed both her eyes and gave a slight nod.

"She picked this one. Do we make a tea from it, too?" He casted a panicked look at Matilda.

"No, a paste for under her tongue," Matilda said calmly. "Saw my mother use it when my grandmother had heart failure. It helps with blood flow." She set about finishing the tea and then started on a paste, speaking to Will while she worked.

"You'd better head back to your truck. Doc'll need help to find the cabin. He should be along soon now."

The doctor's examination was swift, the news not good. "It's heart failure. There's a lot of fluid surrounding her heart. Her medicine might help her feel more comfortable, but I doubt it'll stop a fluid buildup as large as what I hear." He stopped and glanced at Tilly, then back to Will and Matilda. "Did she ever tell either of you she was having chest pain? It's probably been with her for a while."

Both shook their heads. "We haven't known her long, but she never complained of anything," Matilda answered.

"Well, prop her up on some pillows so she can breathe easier. And try to get a little broth in her. She'll need to get nourishment if there's any hope of her making it through this. But don't overload her with too much fluid." Dr. Jennings glanced at Will as he put instruments back into his bag. "Can you lead me out now? And I'll need you to help me back here tomorrow—craziest path I ever tried to follow."

"But Doc...will she make it?" Will's voice trembled. He felt deep affection for this gentle lady who loved the land and his bees as he did. He wanted more time with her.

The doctor's shoulders rose up then dropped down again as he spoke. "It's in God's hands now. Always is, I suppose."

Throughout the long night, they did what they could to make Tilly comfortable. Finally, around dawn, she settled into a deep sleep.

"I think she'll make it," Matilda said, tears filled her eyes.

"Thank God," Will whispered.

Doctor Jennings returned early the next morning, pleased with her improvement, but cautious. "She needs care—plenty of rest and nourishment. I fear it can't happen here."

Will spoke immediately. "She can come to my home. I'll make her a bed in the parlor near the fireplace."

After some struggle, she agreed to come to Applewood Orchard to recuperate. "Only 'til I'm better," she stated emphatically. "I need to be in my woods."

May turned to June with only a few showers to water the earth. Once again, Will worried about his crop. The trees needed rain to produce the best apples. Now the temperatures rose and the weather stayed hot and dry.

He felt unsettled as went through his days doing those things which needed to be done, but with little enthusiasm. Anger still held him captive from the abandonment of his wife.

Will spent each day looking forward to the evening, when he would sit on the floor signing to Lyddie, proud each time she attempted to sign back. She was an amazing child who brought him joy. Everything else left a bitter taste in his mouth.

Tilly tried to talk to Will about his anger, directed at both his wife and God. Finally, in frustration with his stubbornness, she told him, "You can't pick and choose when to follow the Lord. You want to honor him only when times is good. You praise him only in times with no trouble, then get sullen and push him away when things ain't goin' your way. Reckon it's about as dishonoring as you can be."

Her words hurt and stayed with Will long into the night. How could God have let Sybil leave? How could he be left alone with a child with so many needs? How could he honor God when he had so much anger in his heart?

The next night—the night before Tilly planned to go back to her cabin—she spoke again to Will.

"Miz Matilda and Miz Eleanor come to see me today. Told me something amazing."

He stared at her, curious about what could be amazing in her simple life. He waited, hoping Lyddie would allow him to focus his attention on his guest. Often, in the evenings, when he turned his attention to Tilly, Lyddie would toddle over, put her hand on his cheek, and sign "me."

"Night Mr. Carl died, he told Miz Eleanor 'bout a letter wrote by his father, Carl Sr. She found it in the attic at their old place. I reckon I don't wanna tell you why, but old Mr. Rhode left me the eighteen acres between your place and his." She reached and touched his arm. "Hear me out now, and don't go all bull-headed on me. I don't want the land—don't need it. I mean to give it to you—"

"I can't take—" He interrupted, stunned by this turn of events.

"You must take it so you can farm it. Lyddie's goin' to need special teachers, and that'll take money." She paused, then continued. "Miz Matilda's goin' to get the papers fixed up with a lawyer she knows in Lewisburg. But I got a favor. Don't tell nobody how you come by the land. I don't want nobody but us four knowin' I give it to you."

She stopped, taxed by the long speech. After a moment, she spoke again. "There's one more thing. I need your promise on somethin'."

"Anything, Tilly, anything." His heart played strong beats against his ribcage. *The land, the eighteen acres, would be his.*

"The land between us ain't what's important. It's the land of heaven we should be thinkin' on. Bad times'll come, like you know. They do to everybody, I reckon. Promise me you'll hold on fast when it happens and don't never turn your back on God. He plans to bless your life, Mr. Will."

When she finished, tears coursed down both their cheeks. He tried to speak but could only nod. The words of this amazing woman had finally pierced his bitter heart.

Will put the last frame back into the hives when he heard a voice behind him. Turning, he saw Matilda rushing toward him.

"Matilda, stop!" He yelled. "You'll get stung."

She kept advancing. "I've been stung by worse than a little ole' honeybee. Beside they don't like me—I'm too sour."

He smiled. *Nothing could be farther from the truth.* "Well then, what's your hurry?"

"We need to talk, and it can't wait." She puffed from her long walk. "Let's walk back to the fence in the orchard."

Happy to do this, Will led the way. He loved the sight of his land beyond the fence. He itched to improve the old trees and to plant more. *All in good time. I need to get through this Depression.*

"Okay, Matilda, what is it?" He removed his hat and placed one foot on the bottom of the fence.

"Hear me out on this. It may be hard, but I believe you can rise to this occasion."

"Come on, Matilda. When did you ever beat around the bush? Tell me what you came for."

"She's here. Sybil's back. She's on your front porch playing with Lyddie right now."

A rod shot up his spine as he leaned toward Matilda, both feet now on the ground. "Here? Why? And with Lyddie? No, that can't happen." The words spit out, harsh and clipped as he started for the house.

He'd recently found peace with Sybil's absence and had resolved to live without her. But deep in the recesses of his heart still lay a small seed of resentment. Now it burst into life and sent a shoot of indignation through his body.

"Wait, listen first. Then you can do what you want. But you must listen first," Matilda said as she laid a hand on his arm. "Johnny dropped her off at the diner four weeks ago—"

"Four weeks? She's been here a month. Why—"

"Just listen. Emma brought her to me. She seemed broken, Will, yet so peaceful. It must not have been an easy time for her while she was with—"

"Not really my concern, is it now?"

"Will Parson, you will hear me out."

He closed his mouth, wishing he could rush back to his hives and forget what he'd just heard.

"She's changed. Really changed. Something about a tent revival and her new faith. That's for her to share. She wants to come back. But she says if it's not what you want—if you don't come back with me right now—she'll leave and never return."

Matilda waited but got no response.

"You need to know, while Sybil has been with me, she's worked every night with Emma to learn sign language. She's good at it. Better than good. Not as clumsy as the way your hands move. Her fingers can fly."

Will stood silent as every muscle pulled at his bones. Faith, sign language, good at it? The fibers of his mind fired on all cylinders.

Then the soft words of Tilly came back to him. *Don't turn your back on God's blessings. He cares for you.*

Slowly, like honey dripped from a frame, his heart melted. He gave a slight nod to Matilda, not trusting his voice, returned his hat to his head, and stepped toward home.

From the steps of the porch, he watched as his wife signed to Lyddie, his daughter's face entranced. When Sybil glanced at him, he looked into her eyes and signed, "Welcome home."

—END

Book Club Questions

1. "Life will come back to you." What did Big Mama mean by this quote?

2. Which scene stayed with you? Why?

3. Discuss the relationship between the characters and the setting. How does the physical environment reflect the characters' attitude and actions?

4. Which character can you relate to the most? Why?

5. Who would you most like to meet? What would you ask them?

6. Were there places in the story where you wanted more from the author?

7. Do the emotions surrounding abortion come through clearly?

8. How would you describe this author's voice/ writing style?

9. Do you have a favorite quote?

10. This story deals with domestic abuse. Discuss the difference between domestic abuse now and domestic abuse in the 1930s.

11. This story has plenty of tension. Where did you sense it and what was the reason for it?

12. What message(s) do you think the author wanted to convey through this story?

13. Does the title work for you?

14. Did you learn anything about the Great Depression from this story?

15. Forgiveness is a large part of this story. Discuss what each character needed to be forgiven. Did they receive it? From whom?

16. What would you like to ask the author about this book?

Enjoy a sample of *From the Earth*,
the next book in the Wonderful West Virginia
series, on the next pages.

From the Earth

Chapter 1

The loud horn gave three short bursts to signal the end of the workday. Kate rushed to put away the ledgers and gave the desk a quick swipe to remove the coal dust, which settled over everything, even in the offices. Her hands trembled as she screwed the lid on the ink jar with an anxious glance at the door. She grabbed her lunch pail and headed for the door, desperate to escape before the mine's foreman came into the office.

No such luck. He barreled through the door before she reached it.

"Well, Miss Kate. You're in all the hurry today, now ain'cha." Jakub stood so close she could smell the tobacco stored in his left cheek. "You know the rules. You can't leave until the ledgers are checked. I need to know you didn't spend your time in this lonely office dreaming of dresses and boys."

"I entered ten pages today, Mr. Kaminski. Same as every day. The numbers are correct." She turned a shoulder toward the door. "Now, if you'll excuse me, I need to collect my brothers and my sister. Ma doesn't like them to walk home alone."

"That's right. Safety before all else. Mighty big airs your family puts on. Everyone knows your father walks the road like he owns one side of it and plans to buy the other." His upper lip curled as he spoke, making her stomach roll. "Well, the McNaughton family are miners like everyone else in Farrowlee. Time your father acted like it."

Kate pushed past him, barely able to conceal her disdain. Not daring to look back, she walked at a fast clip.

She should've stayed in the coal sorting line, like the other women who worked the mine. Instead, when she turned eighteen, she'd used her good grades and a letter of reference from her teacher to get an office job. Unfortunately, it came with the unwanted attention of Jakub Kaminski.

Away from the offices, she moved toward the large shed where her siblings gathered each day at the end of their shifts. The heat from the late afternoon summer sun felt good on her back. She loved this season, mostly because it made her forget the bone-chilling cold of winter.

"Rudy, Liam, Nessa," Kathleen called to her siblings. As usual, they stood in a tight circle with their friends. "Come now, time to make our way home."

"Ah, Kate. We're just talking about music. There're some great new hits out." Liam said as he gave her a lopsided grin. Of all her siblings, this one could always melt her heart. "Surely you've heard of rock and roll?"

She stuck her hands on her hips. "Now when

would I have time to listen to music, much less the music you kids listen to?" Even though they were all close in age, as the oldest, she assumed a parent's role over her siblings.

Now the three of them were barely recognizable with the black coal grime layered on their faces and arms. It would take a good scrub to remove the soot before the evening meal, and not all of it would come off until their Saturday night bath.

At sixteen, her twin brothers already had the build of a man with broad shoulders and bulging muscles. Fourteen-year-old Nessa started her work on the sorting line earlier this year. Kate wanted her sister to stay in school longer, but Nessa struggled to learn. She suspected her baby sister preferred the mines over the effort it took to navigate through school.

"Let's go. We're already late." Kate moved behind them to herd them home like a sheepdog.

"'Bout time you vagabonds got here," Ma greeted them as they came through the door. "Get washed up. Your father will leave soon."

Ma turned back to the meal she prepared every day for her husband to take down into the coal mine. He worked the night shift, when there were fewer bosses about. William McNaughton rarely took well to being supervised. Kate knew her father bristled every time a boss came around. She worried he'd lose his job because of his acidic mouth.

"Top of the mornin' to ye all!" Da said as he entered the kitchen and pulled a suspender over each shoulder.

His children smiled but said nothing, except for Nessa, who loved to banter. "Da, you know it's almost evening. You really should pay more attention to the time of day!"

"Ah, my darlin', time is about me being Irish. What kind of Irishman would I be if I didn't start the workday with a *top of the mornin'*?"

"The kind that could tell day from night, Da!" Nessa, his kindred spirit, bore his thick black hair and jovial personality.

"Time to stop this foolishness and see your da off to work," Ma said as she put a wrapped bread and butter sandwich in his lunch pail. A boiled sweet potato, a jar of green beans, and a thermos filled with coffee completed his meal.

"Aye, 'tis time, children. Gather round." He waited as his family circled the table once owned by his mother, a wedding gift from her father. They assembled themselves, each reaching for the next one's hand.

"The Lord bless thee and keep thee. The Lord make his face shine upon thee and be gracious unto to thee: the Lord lift up his face upon thee and give thee peace.

"Heavenly Father, watch over this family in their night's sleep and keep me safe as I work to bring your bounty from the earth. Amen."

"So, I'm off to spend time with the mice and all else that roam in the bowels of the mine. May the leprechauns bring you sweet dreams, my lovely family."

Kate watched her father as he ducked below the door frame and left the house whistling. Once again her heart swelled with love for this amazing man who loved his family and worked hard to care for them.

Her heart whispered, *Keep him safe. Bring him back to us.*

The next morning Kate rose with care so as to not wake her sister. Her mind recalled the conversation with Nessa the night before, when they'd settled into their small bed.

"I'll thank you to not be waking me up in the morning. I, sweet sister, have the day off," Nessa announced.

"It's not the good news you think it is, Nessa. The company is only doing this because production is down," Kate replied with a sigh. "They're rotating days off to address the problem, even though the miners' union is fighting against it."

Nessa turned onto her side to face her sister. "Why would the union not like it? I think it's lovely to have a day off during the week."

Kate tweaked her sister's nose. "Because, you little goose, it's a day without pay. Now turn off the light. One of us has to be up early to work."

She lay in the dark for a long time, wondering if the mine might soon start laying off workers. With two more small children at home, the McNaughton family needed the income they collectively provided.

Most days, Kate ate her lunch from a lunch pail filled each morning. But today, she made a quick trip home for the noon meal, drawn by the thought of fresh bread's aroma sure to fill the house. She could already taste a slice slathered with butter.

She hurried through the door, expecting to be engulfed by a tantalizing smell. When nothing hit her nose, disappointment rose from her hungry stomach. "Ma, what's wrong? Where's the bread?"

"It's Nessa. I sent her to buy flour ages ago. She hasn't come back. I can't leave the wee ones to go find her." Ma opened and closed her hands as if she were kneading dough.

"I'll go find her. Don't worry. She probably found a friend to talk to." She wished she believed what she'd said to her mother. Her heart raced at the thought of the many things that could happen—all of which turned her blood cold.

She hurried to the main street of Farrowlee, intending to start at the company store. *Mr. O'Leary will know what time she left—if she made it there at all.*

The scene inside the store stopped her cold. Nessa stood before the baking goods, tears streaming from red, swollen eyes. Beside her stood a large black man.

"Mr. O'Leary, you should separate the bags of flour from the bags of sugar. Last time I confused them and purchased the wrong one," the man said with a chuckle as he reached for the flour. "This is the one I need. Please put it and this box of soap flakes on my tab." He held the bag in his hands for a moment, then walked out the back door of the store after he gave Kate a slight nod.

Nessa reached out a trembling hand to take hold of a bag from where the man had grabbed his. She turned to her sister with questioning eyes. Kate flew to her side.

She nodded to indicate Nessa had made the correct choice, then walked over to the counter.

"What happened?" she asked the storekeeper.

"Not sure I can say," Finn responded. "Your sister's been standing there almost since I opened this morning. I tried to get her to tell me why, but she didn't seem to hear me." He sighed and lowered his voice. "I wanted to help her but didn't know how. Saddest thing I've ever seen."

"Who's that man? And why did he stand next Nessa?"

"His name is Isaac Johnson. He'll be the new teacher at the black school when summer is over. Hasn't been here long." The storekeeper paused. "He'd just moved over to where Nessa stood when you walked in."

She had more questions about the man but knew it best not to show interest in him. "Please put the flour on our tab. I'll get her home," she said, then walked back to where Nessa still stood. She put a gentle arm around her sister as they walked out the front door of the store.

Chapter 2

Caitlin hurried up the steep trail, eager to be home before Henry arrived at the end of his workday. It would never do for him to know she walked from their home high on the hill to Farrowlee each day. She enjoyed the daily walk, although it did little to abate her loneliness. The postman handed her the mail in silence. The storekeeper offered her polite conversation, but his son seemed frightened to speak to the mine superintendent's wife.

Her husband announced upon their arrival that she was not to go into the company town. "The miners and their families are beneath us. You should never try to befriend them."

She inwardly chuckled each time Henry used the phrase *beneath us* since their ornate home did indeed sit high on the hill above the cluster of miner's homes and the few shops in Farrowlee.

Caitlin disregarded Henry's directive. For the three months they'd been in Farrowlee, she walked to the post office and the company store Mondays through Fridays instead of having Mr. O'Leary's son deliver their mail and groceries. Each day, she returned home disappointed, as no one except Mr. O'Leary attempted to be friendly to her. The poverty and desolation she saw in town disturbed her. Surely the company could do something about it.

Today, she'd seen two young girls hurry from the company store, girls near to her age. How she longed to talk with another woman. Yet, they ducked their heads when they saw her and hurried on. At least she had a letter from Aunt Matilda. She'd get the Berkley news and perhaps hear how Lyddie was doing.

Lyddie Anne Parson had been her closest friend since the day Caitlin arrived at her Aunt Matilda's as a six-year-old, scared to meet a relative she'd never seen and filled with grief from the loss of her parents, who'd been killed in a car accident. Lyddie helped her through the difficult time. Her deafness came with a quiet peace—a salve to Caitlin's wounded heart. Over time, Caitlin learned sign language from Lyddie's parents, and a strong bond of friendship grew between her and Lyddie.

Back home, she threw the mail on the table in the spacious foyer, then hurried to the kitchen to put on her apron. The stew she'd made earlier simmered on the stove. She put a pan of cornbread in the oven, thankful for Aunt Matilda who insisted she learn to cook. Caitlin often balked at the idea of more time in the kitchen when she'd much rather be outdoors to roam the woods with her yellow dog, Missy. She smiled now, recalling the many compliments Henry gave her when they finished a meal.

She'd just set the table when she thought of the letter. She hurried to the foyer and stuffed it in her apron pocket. She'd read it when Henry went to sleep. Caitlin didn't want him to see the emotions letters from home brought.

"I'm home. Where's my bride?" Henry laid his hat on the foyer table and grabbed the mail. Sifting through it, he laid it back on the table as his wife came into sight.

"She's right here, although not really a bride any longer." Caitlin smiled at the man who captured her heart when he came from England to Berkley, West Virginia to assess the viability of finding new veins of coal in the mine. They'd met at church on a chilly fall morning. Aunt Matilda, who loved to entertain, invited him for Sunday dinner.

Before he left, he asked Caitlin to take a walk the next afternoon. "I've never seen fall foliage like this anywhere except in these beautiful mountains." He glanced at the dog sitting near Caitlin's feet. "Missy told me she'd love a walk in the woods." His beautiful smile and charming accent prompted her to accept the invitation.

She fell in love with Henry Carter, a well-educated man who held an important job in the coal industry. He enjoyed nature as much as she did. The next several months were a whirlwind of courtship and finally a proposal.

Things became even busier, as her aunt insisted a bride must have a trousseau. There were many trips to Lewisburg for clothes and household goods, and even to Charleston to buy the wedding dress. Aunt Matilda increased the cooking lessons, which left Caitlin little time to be with Lyddie.

They married in May at Aunt Matilda's church. It had been an ornate wedding with an abundance of flowers and crowded pews full of guests. Lyddie, her only bridesmaid, looked lovely in her long pink dress with a cinched waist and a full skirt of tulle.

Henry asked Lyddie's father, Will, to be his best man. He stood next to the groom and signed the ceremony to his daughter, who watched his hands as tears streamed down her cheeks. Caitlin didn't know if they were tears of joy for the wedding, or tears of sorrow because her best friend would leave after the wedding reception for a new home in southern West Virginia.

Three weeks before the wedding, Henry announced he'd been offered the superintendent's position at Farrowlee, a small mining town five hours from Berkley. "It's a wonderful opportunity, Caitlin," he said the night he told her about the new position. "My own mine. And you'll be a superintendent's wife."

A superintendent's wife? He made it sound like she'd have a job as well. Fear grabbed her at the thought. She tried to share Henry's excitement while hiding her fears and the pain of leaving Aunt Matilda and others she loved.

She watched as her husband devoured the meal as though it might disappear at any moment. How could this gentle and proper man become such a carnivore at mealtime? Aunt Matilda taught her much about keeping a home, but little about life with a man. She smiled as she waited for him to come to the end of the bowl of stew, then ventured cautiously into a conversation.

"Henry, it's easy to see the poverty in Farrowlee. Does the mining company do anything to help these people?"

His jaw tightened. When he put down the spoon with a force stronger than necessary, she wished she could take back the words.

"It's their own choice. They can leave anytime if they think they can get a better job elsewhere." He spewed out his words, making her flinch.

Questions flew around in her head as she desperately wanted to know more about those living near her. But she remained silent as she gazed at her half-eaten dinner, fearful any more questions would give evidence of her daily trips to Farrowlee.

"We might help more, but the labor unions keep us busy with their requests—which are many." Henry paused, shaking his head. "There are union strikes and even violence at mines all over the country. I spent most of today with union officials who made threats of a strike right here. Stubborn bunch of men! They were pushing for higher pay, better housing, even breaks in the morning and the afternoon. Now I ask you, what would that do to our profits? Don't talk to me about their poverty. They can take two shifts if they need more money." He rose, throwing his napkin on the table. "I'm just trying to keep a lid on a boiling pot."

Their first disagreement. A single tear tracked down her cheek as she watched her husband retreat to the parlor to spend time with his pipe and his newspaper.

The tension remained throughout the evening, nothing like the ones they usually enjoyed, which were filled with conversation and laughter. Relieved when bedtime finally came, Caitlin waited until Henry began snoring before she slipped from the bed and made her way to the kitchen. She pulled the letter from the apron pocket hanging on a peg in the kitchen and sat down at the small table near the sink. The beautiful cursive handwriting so distinct to Aunt Matilda made her smile.

Dear Caitlin,

It's hard to believe it's been three months since your marriage. The town is still talking about the wedding. I hope it was everything you dreamed of. And now, my prayer is for you to find great contentment in your marriage and in your new life. I have so many questions—too many to put in a letter. What's it like to be a superintendent's wife? What's the town of Farrowlee like? Have you made any friends? Your letters offer little information. I hope to come see you soon so I can get the answers I long for.

Now, sweetheart, it is time for me to tell you the purpose of this letter. Our Tilly went to be with the Lord last week. She died peacefully in her bed at the cabin she loved.

Caitlin forced her fist against her mouth as sobs rose from her body. Tilly, gone? Floods of memories returned in a flash—the many times this gentle woman had patiently shown her and Lyddie the wonders of the forest. She'd taught them to respect what God had created.

Often, Tilly led them through the forest, identifying the flora. Through her, the pair of girls, one silent, the other chatty, learned how to press flowers. They eventually put their collection into a large notebook, then meticulously recorded the name of each bloom.

Her next thought went to Lyddie. Tilly had been a special friend who had once saved her life and offered many hours of companionship as Lyddie tried to navigate a hearing world. *Oh, Lyddie, how you must miss her.*

She blinked away her tears and continued reading.

I shall miss her greatly, especially the times we shared coffee and her incredible biscuits. I'm so thankful for her friendship. She seemed to be the only person in Berkley who had any wisdom. Our time together filled me with a love of God and his creation, which I may have gone through this life never knowing.

The Parson family will miss her also, especially Lyddie and her young brother Luke. Tilly had become Luke's special friend, introducing him to her forest much as she did with you.

I'm sorry this letter brings such sad news. Be comforted to know she had a beautiful funeral held at the church she loved. Will buried her at the edge of his orchard, near the beehives she helped him tend.

Please write soon, sweet niece. I miss you.
With love,
Matilda

Caitlin held the letter against her heart as emotions swirled through her. What did she have to share about her new life? Loneliness and deceit had become her only companions.

Acknowledgments

My heartfelt appreciation goes out to those listed below and to the many others who encouraged me and celebrated with me along the way.

Thank you to my Lord, who blessed me with the opportunity to write this story and continues to bless me with His presence every day.

Thank you to the wonderful people of West Virginia, who patiently answered my questions and helped light a fire in me to write this story. Special thanks to Peggy McCracken at the Beckley Exhibition Mine Museum, for sharing her family's history about mining; and to Jason Murphy from Hive House Bees for explaining bee keeping and allowing me to watch the harvest of a swarm.

Thank you to WOWG—my amazing writing group who helped me with every step of the process.

Thank you to Christy Shelsy, my writing

accountability partner. Our weekly sessions kept me at my computer, so I'd be ready for our time together.

And finally, thank you to my husband for believing in me.

Brenda O'Bannion is an author and a retired teacher. She is a member of the American Christian Fiction Writers and the Water Oak Writing Group. She has previously published three children's books and a novel.

She currently lives with her husband in Georgetown, Texas where she enjoys her book club friends, volunteering at the public library, and teaching in Sunday School.

Brenda's books:

Crowbaby and Dawfie is a moving book about an autistic child.

Patchwork Annie is a children's book that uses wordplay to spin a delightful story with a surprise twist at the end.

Her chapter book ***What's Up, Cody?*** addresses the subject of childhood bullying in a way helpful to youngsters.

By and By, I Reckon is a creative parallel memoir in which the connection between Brenda and her grandmother Leola spills out in similar stories of poverty, love, faith, and resilience.

Brenda's website: www.riverroadbooks.com.

Made in the USA
Coppell, TX
26 July 2022

80464883R00163